Showtime!

My day started out like usual—you know, wake up, shower . . . have two hairdressers do my hair. A makeup artist do my face. Some professional fashionista put clothes on me.

No, that's *not* a regular morning.

"Cameras . . . rolling!" the words rang across the studio. The crowd cheered, and the television in the corner of the room where I was waiting suddenly came to life. MORA LIVE! flashed across the screen. I watched as Mora—yes, *that* Mora, Queen of All Talk Shows—made her way on to the stage.

"My guest today certainly needs little introduction," Mora said. "If you have a teenage daughter, she probably faked a fever today so she could stay home and watch this show. Making her national TV debut on *Mora Live!* . . . Jamie Bartlett!"

OK, this is the point where my mom yells to wake me out of my daydream that I'm famous, right?

Nope. It isn't a daydream. It's really happening to me. That's right, thanks, I know, you loved my book. Yeah, I was pretty surprised to knock the wizard boy off number one.

It's me, Jamie Bartlett. The bestselling author of the year.

★

OTHER BOOKS YOU MAY ENJOY

*How My Private,
Personal Journal
Became a Bestseller*

How my

PRIVATE, PERSONAL

Journal

PUFFIN BOOKS

became

a

Bestseller

A NOVEL
BY
**JULIA
DeVILLERS**

PUFFIN BOOKS

Published by the Penguin Group

Penguin Young Readers Group, 345 Hudson Street, New York, New York 10014, U.S.A.

Penguin Group (Canada), 90 Eglinton Avenue East, Suite 700, Toronto, Ontario, Canada M4P 2Y3 (a division of Pearson Penguin Canada Inc.)

Penguin Books Ltd, 80 Strand, London WC2R 0RL, England

Penguin Ireland, 25 St Stephen's Green, Dublin 2, Ireland (a division of Penguin Books Ltd)

Penguin Group (Australia), 250 Camberwell Road, Camberwell,

Victoria 3124, Australia (a division of Pearson Australia Group Pty Ltd)

Penguin Books India Pvt Ltd, 11 Community Centre, Panchsheel Park, New Delhi - 110 017, India

Penguin Group (NZ), Cnr Airborne and Rosedale Roads, Albany, Auckland 1310, New Zealand (a division of Pearson New Zealand Ltd)

Penguin Books (South Africa) (Pty) Ltd, 24 Sturdee Avenue,

Rosebank, Johannesburg 2196, South Africa

Registered Offices: Penguin Books Ltd, 80 Strand, London WC2R 0RL, England

Published in the United States of America by Dutton Children's Books,
a division of Penguin Young Readers Group, 2004

Published by Puffin Books, a division of Penguin Young Readers Group, 2005

10 9 8 7 6 5 4 3 2 1

THE LIBRARY OF CONGRESS HAS CATALOGED THE DUTTON EDITION AS FOLLOWS:

DeVillers, Julia.

How my private, personal journal became a bestseller

by Julia DeVillers.—1st ed.

p. cm.

Summary: A young woman accidentally turns in a private story from her journal instead of an English assignment and becomes a bestselling author almost overnight.

ISBN 0-525-47283-5

[1. Authors—Fiction. 2. High schools—Fiction. 3. Schools—Fiction.
4. Diaries—Fiction.]

I. Title. PZ7.D4974Ho 2004 [Fic]—dc22 2003021568

Puffin Books ISBN 0-14-240332-6

Printed in the United States of America

To Robin Rozines, my mom

"Thirty seconds! *Thirty seconds until showtime, everyone!!*"

I shifted around, trying to get comfortable. You'd think a TV talk show would have a comfortable chair for their guests. I mean, some of the hugest celebrities in the world had sat on this *exact* chair. And they were probably not comfortable, either.

"Teeth check!" Diana moved in front of my face for a close-up check. Diana was my media coach. Diana's brochure said she could help you "Be Your Best on TV!" I was her newest client. And probably about to be her worst failure.

I bared my teeth at her. Not that there would be any food caught in them. I'd been too freaked out to eat anything since I woke up.

My day started out like usual—you know, wake up, shower . . . have two hairdressers do my hair. A makeup artist do my face. Some professional fashionista put clothes on me.

No, that's *not* a regular morning. I did have to admit, I looked pretty good for me. My shoulder-length, dirty blond hair, for once not stringy and split end-y. My best feature, my big green eyes, highlighted in purpley shadow by the make-up artist. My underdeveloped body camouflaged in a blue dress.

"Ten seconds!"

"Chin up, Jamie, stop looking down, you're messing up your hair," Diana hissed. "Do your grounding breath!" I tried some of the breathing methods she claimed would prevent me from passing out in front of twenty million viewers.

"Cameras . . . rolling!" the words rang across the studio. The crowd cheered, and the television in the corner of the room where I was waiting suddenly came to life. MORA LIVE! flashed across the screen. I watched as Mora—yes, *that* Mora, Queen of All Talk Shows—made her way on to the stage.

"My guest today certainly needs little introduction," Mora said. "If you have a teenage daughter, she probably faked a fever today so she could stay home and watch this show."

Diana put her hands on my shoulders, careful not to mess up my hair those two hairdressers had slaved over. She gave me a quick massage.

"Jamie, loosen up! Think about something that makes you smile! Think about Justin Timberlake!" she said.

Justin Timberlake, Justin Timberlake. Justin, Justin. I love Justin. That should make me smile, right? But I suddenly thought of something. What if Justin Timberlake was sitting home resting up after some concert and all-night party and he's turning on the TV and *Mora Live!* is on and he's about to watch me?! What was I even doing here? Right now I was supposed to be in English, passing notes to Harmony, staring at Marco Vega. Good thing Marco Vega wasn't watching me on TV. That would *really* freak me out. Wait. What if he *was* watching me? What if Miss Gallagher, my English teacher, had rolled one of those TV monitors into the classroom? And the whole class was staring at the screen waiting to see . . .

"Making her national TV debut on *Mora Live!* . . . Jamie Bartlett!"

OK. I'm on. Move legs: left, right, left. Walking, walking up the steps to the stage, remembering Diana's instructions.

I made eye contact with the audience as best as I could, considering there were these massive lights shining directly into my eyes. I smiled at the first girl I could see in the front row. She looked ten times cooler than me. And OMG, that totally cool girl started waving at me and crying.

OMG OMG OMG.

OK, this is the point where my mom yells to wake me out of my daydream that I'm famous, right?

Nope. It isn't a daydream. It's really happening to me. That's right, thanks, I know, you loved my book. Yeah, I was pretty surprised to knock the wizard boy off number one.

It's me, Jamie Bartlett. The bestselling author of the year.

POP QUIZ:

Q: So how does one totally average high school girl with a B+ in English become a bestselling author freaking out on *Mora Live!*?

A: It all started one night last fall. Harmony, my BFF, was hanging out in my room, per usual. We were doing what we do so well. Our nails.

~

I was sitting on my bed, dipping and painting, using magazines to lay my fingers on while they dried.

"'Out of five hundred teens and tweens polled, eighty-four percent included lip gloss as one of the three most crucial items to have if stranded on a deserted island,'" Harmony read from one of the magazine pages. "Who writes this garbage?" She threw the magazine across the room.

"Watch out," I warned. Too late.

"Shoot, I smudged," said Harmony, examining her hand. "Thumb, take two."

"Check out Amber Tiffany." I pointed to the cover of the magazine lying under my newly OoLaLaLavender nails. "How is it humanly possible for someone to look like that?"

"It's *not* humanly possible," Harmony said, in her best *It's a burden having such a naive and foolish best friend, but it's my mission to enlighten her* voice. "Amber Tiffany is airbrushed. She's the result of trick lighting and a year's worth of our allowance in makeup and skin care. Plus graphic designers sit around and cover up her zits with a zillion-dollar computer program. And *look* at her. She probably has more plastic in her body than Barbie."

"Yeah, yeah, and blah blah blah. Even with all of that, I would still never look good enough for Marco Vega to even recognize my existence." I flopped back on my bed. No response. I sighed loudly for extra drama.

"James, your looks are totally fine. However, your standards are unrealistic and shallow. Now put that magazine down," Harmony said. I saw her notice the orange Post-it note I'd stuck on my mirror that said, *"English essay due Tuesday!"*

"Hey," Harmony said, "what'd you write your essay about?"

I blew on my nail polish. I didn't want to think about English class right now. And not only because I hadn't written the essay yet. But because Sawyer Sullivan was in that class, too.

And I got Sawyered today.

I was walking into class when Sawyer came in behind me with her friends.

Sawyer looked me up and down. She rolled her eyes.

"Nice outfit," she said. "If you're color-blind."

And her friends started laughing. Ha. Ha. Ha.

I tried to look at them with a little smile like, *No big deal. Doesn't bother me*.

"What are *you* looking at?" Sawyer asked me. "Stare much?"

I shuddered. OK, let's think about something else now, shall we? I turned back to my magazine.

"Look at this. My thigh is bigger than her waist," I moaned, as I looked at one of the models. OK, that really wasn't so true. If I had any complaints, it was that my body was too small. As in short, undeveloped, no sign of anything happening, anywhere. But you know, everyone complains about being too fat. Everyone does, so hey.

Well, everyone except Harmony.

"That does it." Harmony gave me the look. "If you cannot stop comparing yourself to every model in those magazines, then I must take drastic measures. Say 'Buh-bye magazines.'" One big swoop and she lifted them up and tossed them in the garbage can.

"Hey! I didn't read the article on Amber Tiffany's secrets to soft, full lips!" I yelped.

Harmony picked up her backpack and her new laptop. Harmony now had two—yes, two—laptops. The new one was a guilt gift from her mother since her birthday fell on the "upstate" month this year. Harmony splits her time between New York City and her dad's place here in upstate New York suburbia.

We can take a train to NYC. That's where Harmony's mom and stepfather live. And, every other month, that's where Harmony lives, too. One month upstate, one month in the city. That's her life. We live too far for her to commute to school, so I barely see her during city months. I'm always so happy when it's Harmony's month to live up here.

Except maybe right now. She's getting naggy.

"One more time—did you even *start* your English paper?" Harmony asked, pulling my Post-it note down. "Tuesday is tomorrow, you know."

"Well, no," I confessed. "Don't worry. I'll whip something off. As soon as I find out Amber Tiffany's secret to soft, full lips. I'll even share the secret with you."

Harmony stuck the Post-it note to my forehead.

"I don't even want to know," Harmony said. "I'm taking off. You want to use my new laptop? It's got some cool fonts on it."

"Thanks!" I said, taking it. She was so lucky. I had to fight for time on our ancient computer with Allie, my older sister.

"If you want, email me your essay later. I'll print it out for you on my new color laser printer," Harmony said. "Get you a couple bonus points for neatness."

2

I sat on my bed and opened Harmony's laptop. It was nice and shiny and new. Almost made me want to start writing on it.

Almost. Because ugh.

I hate writing for school. Writing for a teacher sucks the life out of it—you can't really express yourself. Try to be original? Hah. Your teacher's goal is to plow through as many papers as he possibly can without having to think. Originality throws off the game plan. Then there's the whole boring way you have to set things up. Introduction, body, conclusion, sources in exact bibliographic style. You know the deal.

But, like a good little Whittaker High student, I write what teachers want to read and turn in my assignments on time.

And I go home and bang out my journals.

I journal almost every day. And that's the kind of writing I love to do. When it's for myself. When it's my feelings, my thoughts. Instead of using diaries or pretty little journals that scream, NOSY SISTERS READ IMMEDIATELY!, I ingeniously write in regular school notebooks marked "Algebra" and "History." My sister doesn't even open her *own* school notebooks. So I know my journals are for my eyes only.

OK, back to homework. We had to write an essay about something we would do to change the world.

I cranked out a paper on how I would change the breaks between classes. Yes, having longer breaks between classes would change the world because we would have time to actually go to our lockers and switch our books so we didn't have to lug around sixty pounds of backpack all day. And that would give us all better posture, something always being drilled into our brains in health class.

It was actually brilliant because rumor had it that Gallagher was dating Mr. "Anatomy" Akins, the health teacher. So she could cozy up to him by telling him how one of her students thought his lessons were so great she wrote about it in her homework. Two teachers, inspiring their students together. How romantic. (Gag.)

Homework done. Over. Great. Now I could journal. I started to close the laptop, but then I noticed the new program installed on Harmony's hard drive. It was the one that made text look like it was written in glitter gel. I'm a gel-pen junkie. Now I could be a hi-tech gel-pen junkie, too. I would just type my journal entry, print it later, and glue it in my notebook for a special effect.

OK, what to journal about . . . hm . . . .

I rolled over on my back. Models from magazines stared

back at me from my ceiling and walls. A couple months ago I redecorated my room. I talked my mom into tossing my pink-and-white gingham comforter and pillows I'd had since I was five. I snagged a denim comforter from the guest room. It was pretty weak redecorating. But I just wasn't feeling pink gingham anymore. Then I got a box and took everything off my shelves: a good citizenship trophy, the princess figurines, an award I won at summer camp. I pulled down my collage of old pictures of me on a horse, me on vacation at the beach, me and Allie, back when we were on speaking terms. I had piled all my Beanie Babies into the box, too. Even my favorite, the purple unicorn with the sparkly horn.

I'd redecorated using all my teen magazines. My bedroom was now the Land of the Beautiful People. Present company excluded, of course. Pictures of models, glam, gorgeous, thin, dressed in perfect clothes, having the best time ever. The way I wanted my life to be. The way *I* wanted to be.

All right, all right, we all know it isn't as good as it looks. Harmony's right: You know that, I know that. Some of those models and celebrities are screwed-up, married a million times, in rehab, tossing down the pills or yakking it up in the ladies' room to stay that thin.

OK, but you don't see me ripping down the pictures, do you? Yup, I'm a major hypocrite. Because I know those pictures aren't real life. But I still want to look like Amber Tiffany!

I guess my room has the opposite effect on me than I wanted. It's hard to feel pretty when a ceiling full of über-humans is staring at you. Like they are looking at you and thinking, *Thank the lord I don't have your butt.* And, *I have such great breasts I am going to shove them in your face, you flat-chested freak.*

Why can't I stop comparing myself to them? Why is it Me vs. Amber Tiffany? Me vs. the actresses, the supermodels, the girls dancing around in the music videos. . . . Why can't I think my body is normal and OK?

I know there are girls out there thinking the same thing. Why couldn't we just stop?!?!?!

You know what, I was sick of it. Staring at those models, those actresses, those girls in the music videos—and questioning myself.

Journal time.

I started to type. I pounded out my pissiness into a story. I named the main character Isabella. Isabella would have long, golden, glossy straight hair. No, delete that: too stereotype Barbie. Isabella was going to fit no stereotype. She would have long, dark, wild, curly hair that she would shake around with total confidence. Isabella was curvy. Not stick thin, not model perfect. And strong and athletic. Graceful, too. *She* never got politely asked to skip Junior Ballet class the day the newspaper came to write a story about it.

Isabella wore great clothes. OK, the point is that looks shouldn't count. I know, I know. But she's *my* dream girl, and there's nothing wrong with having style. Isabella had her favorite stores at the mall, like me. But she'd also go into vintage shops, where she would spend, like, twenty-five dollars and come out with an incredible outfit. Yeah, and she would buy a pair of regular jeans and do-it-herself until they were cooler than even designer jeans.

Isabella liked to lie around and paint her nails and read magazines. But when *she* read the magazines, she didn't give one thought to the body the clothes were hanging on. She would just think, hm, this would look great on me—it is so my personal style. Isabella is TOTALLY FINE being herself.

And that's not all.

Isabella would become a real superhero. She would have an alter ego. Like Clark Kent becomes Superman! Like Peter Parker becomes Spider-Man! Like the little wimpy guy becomes the Incredible Hulk! Most of the time Isabella is this seriously cool girl. But when the Evil Villains attack, Isabella turns into . . .

IS!!!

OK, so IS should have some cool superpowers, right? I thought of how Wonder Woman had those bracelet things on her arms that warded off the villains. And how Buffy staked the vampires. I had a sudden inspiration. Isabella would make a fist! And Flick! She would flick open her fingers and spread positivity rays that would protect her from Evil! Yes, the Flick could only be used for Good!

Of course, IS needed an evil nemesis. The ultimate villain to fight in a showdown. A girl of Supreme Evil. I'd call her Bertha. No, Myrna. Yeah, Myrna. Look out, Myrna, Reigning-Bitchy-Girl-at-School-Supermodel-Celebrity-It Girl to the Extreme! You are about to reign no more!

(Myrna turned out to be a totally hateable villain. Myrna also bore a sneaking resemblance to one Sawyer Sullivan . . . heh!)

I started the story with this girl getting made fun of by Myrna. The girl isn't model perfect. Her fashion sense is a little lacking. She's an ordinary girl. Myrna is rolling her eyes at her, saying things like "Nice outfit. If you're color-blind!" That kind of thing. Totally laughing at her. And the girl's feeling hopeless! Helpless! Oh no, right?! This poor girl! But then . . . suddenly . . .

IS slid off the unicorn's back and stood face-to-face with Myrna.

"What are you looking at?" Myrna sneered. "Stare much?"

IS looked Myrna right in the eye. Then she held up her fist.

FLICK!

Myrna flew backward into the air. CRASH! Myrna sprawled on the ground.

"Hey!" Myrna yelled. "You messed up my hair! You chipped my nail polish!"

IS just ignored her.

"Who do you think you are?!" Myrna hissed at her.

"I am IS."

And Myrna ran away.

OK, of course Myrna wouldn't give up that quickly. She'd run to her lair and plan IS's demise. Myrna was the Leader of a force of evil villains. Like Mojo Jojo, Dr. Drakken, or Skeletor . . .

I called them . . . The Evil Clique of Populors!

The Backstabbor!
The Gossipor!
The Insultor!
The Fashionistor!
The Ostracizor!
The Dietor!
The Betrayor!

So IS would have to fight all of those guys and then . . . in a final showdown . . . IS would face her nemesis, Myrna.

And of course, IS would win. It wouldn't be easy. But ohhhh yes! Myrna and her society of perfect-supermodel-brainwashed lackeys would be going down! IS would rise up and make things the way they should be! For all of us not-model-perfect-not-flat-bellied-not-huge-chesty NORMAL and NICE girls!

I wrote and wrote. I lost myself in the writing and just let it all out. I wrapped my red polar-fleece blanket around my shoulders and poured my feelings on to the laptop. IS wasn't going to take it anymore. IS knew what we faced. But she actually did something about it—something that really, really worked. Oh wow, did it work.

My parents stopped in to say good night, but I barely looked up. My fingers ached from typing, but I couldn't seem to stop. I finished sometime around midnight. Then I remembered I hadn't emailed Harmony my essay for Gallagher's class, so I sent that to her.

I finally turned off the laptop. I was beat. I crawled into bed, and crashed hard.

~

Myrna called an emergency meeting of her Evil Clique of Populors.

"Her name is IS," Myrna announced. "Her full range of powers is yet unknown. But know this, My Superior Villainesses: IS must be stopped."

3

POP QUIZ:

**What is the most potentially excruciating
part of the school day?**

A. Math
B. Gym
C. Health
D. Lunch

It's pretty close. I mean math, there's that chance you might fall asleep and drool all over your desk. And gym—if your school has a pool, you really know what I mean. Health? You try listening to Mr. "Anatomy" Akins explain sex education. Yikes. But the answer is D) Lunch. Because if it's bad—it's BAD.

Lunch is a sociological study of high school. Where you sit + who you sit with = who you are. The worst thing to happen in school on a regular basis is to have no one to sit with during lunch. And yes, it happened to me last year in eighth. I've almost blacked it out of my memory: walking into the cafeteria the first day of school, looking around and seeing nobody . . . nobody . . . still nobody. Well, yeah, there were people I *knew*. But no one was waving or smiling and saying, "Hi, are you the new girl? Wanna sit with us?"

BECAUSE I WAS NOT THE NEW GIRL! At least if I *was* the new girl, I would know that I was standing there not knowing where to go because I was new. But, no, I had gone to school with some of these people all my life. It was just that they were already grouped off, and you can't go crashing lunch tables without being invited.

So I begged the librarian to let me spend the period as a library aide. The whole year I scarfed down my lunch between the shelves while putting books in their proper Dewey Decimal homes. It was *still* better than sitting alone at lunch.

This year's lunch period almost makes up for last year's disaster. Harmony has the same lunch, and so does my friend Lindsay.

I was a little tired after being up so late last night. Harmony had printed off my paper for Gallagher's class *and* turned it in for me with hers during homeroom to snag the bonus points for early submission.

"Thanks for turning in my paper," I said to Harmony. I admired her outfit. Harmony always looked amazing. Isabella's style ideas? I got a lot of them from Harmony. She would take a white T-shirt and use scissors or ribbons or lace or whatever and invent something amazing. That day she was wearing a denim jacket she'd dyed and patched up herself, one of her original T's, and cargos. It went perfectly with her dark skin, huge eyes, and braided-up dark hair.

As for me, well. I tried. I spent hours inhaling fashion magazines. I tried to look trendy. I checked out what Sawyer Sullivan and the other popular girls wore and tried to match it. But, somehow, I just didn't get it right. Lindsay didn't even bother. Some might say she was something of a fashion emergency. But she didn't really care about clothes much. She was just into being comfy. Today she had on a baggy sweatshirt and track pants, with her medium-length curly reddish hair kind of crazy.

Lindsay pointed across the room.

Kelsey Gibbs and Dylan Sanders were making out all over the place.

"Get a room," Harmony said.

"So, how come *we're* all boyfriend-less?" I complained.

"Me, because I'm fat," Lindsay said.

"Hey!" Harmony shot back at her. "I told you I don't want to hear you talking like that."

"Well, Jamie asked . . . ," Lindsay whined.

"You are *not* fat," I said, for the billionth time. Then I pointed to Olivia Roberts sitting with her boyfriend. "Besides, size doesn't mean someone can't get a boyfriend. Cody worships the ground Olivia walks on."

"We just haven't found the right guys yet," Harmony said.

Harmony was notoriously picky. I'd suggested every guy in school and nope, not for her.

"Well, *I've* found the right one for me," I said. "And here he is!"

Marco Vega had entered the cafeteria.

Marco Vega was another plus to this year's lunch population. Food *and* a view. Ah. His jet-black hair, his chocolate-brown eyes, his muscled arms carrying his lunch tray of scary cafeteria food. Ah.

He was so . . . so . . . hot.

I'd been crushing on Marco Vega since last year. I used to think he was your garden-variety hottie. You know: Nice outside. Not much inside.

Until this day last year in English. Mr. Bleemos had us partner up and read our homework assignments out loud to each other. Marco Vega was my partner. And the assignment had been to write a poem.

Marco read his poem to me . . . a love poem. It was about the intensity of longing for true love. About depth and heart-breaking beauty. The quest for just the right love to set you free.

Such depth! Such passion! All waiting under the surface to be set free.

And I wanted to be the one to set it free.

"Wow!" I told Marco when he had finished reading his poem. That was about all I could say without flinging myself at him.

He looked into my eyes. And he goes, "Oh . . . it was nothing. Don't spread that around, okay?"

OK, he didn't want anyone to know he wrote poetry. Probably thought it would ruin his image. Oh yes. I would keep it our little secret.

That was the last time I'd talked to Marco Vega. But I worshipped him from afar.

Mostly from far across the cafeteria.

"Marco Vega is a god," I breathed. "Do you think if I stare at him long enough he would look this way?"

On cue, Marco looked over and we all squealed and ducked. OK, only I squealed and ducked. Oh, yeah, I'm smoooooth.

"Hey, Jamie, what'd you write your paper for Gallagher's class about?" Harmony asked a little too loudly, probably on purpose to stop me from staring and drooling.

But before I could answer, Sawyer Sullivan spoke up. "Oh, you'll find out this afternoon what Jamie wrote."

Sawyer was sitting at the table behind us. She was a definite minus in the lunch-period situation. Sawyer was sitting close enough so she could hear every word we said, but a universe away in school status. You know a Sawyer—we all have that misfortune. Sawyer and her friends were the staple group of every high school clique system. The girls at the top. The populars, the stars, the cheerleaders, the ones who got the cutest guys, wore the best clothes—all that. I've heard rumors that in some schools, the Popular Clique actually is made up of nice, friendly girls. Lucky them. It definitely wasn't that way at Whittaker. Our Popular Group were witches with a capital B.

"Please bless us with your wisdom," Harmony said sweetly.

Sawyer ignored her. "Gallagher's going to read Jamie's paper out loud to the class this afternoon." Sawyer was Miss Gallagher's teacher's aide. Her sucking up probably guaranteed her a higher grade.

"Gallagher thinks Jamie's paper is, let's see if I can remember this right from what she told Mr. Akins while she was gazing into his eyes," Sawyer continued. "'The most provocative paper she has seen in her fifteen years of teaching.' Puh-lease. Like *Jamie Bartlett* has something interesting to say?"

Sawyer's groupies laughed like she had said something incredibly hilarious and turned back to chatting amongst themselves before they went over their talking-to-nonpopular-people quota. To add to my pain, Marco Vega came over and plopped down practically on Sawyer's lap.

Did I mention that Marco and Sawyer are going out? No. Forgive me, I try to forget that myself.

"White bubble, white bubble," Harmony muttered under her breath to help me out. Harmony is into yoga and meditation. See, Harmony told me that if you imagine a white bubble around you, then all the negativity will just bounce off the surface and not affect you. It seemed to work for her.

Harmony looks like she should be in Sawyer's group and was even recruited back in seventh. Sawyer and the Jennifers approached Harmony all formally and Sawyer goes, "We are going to the mall after school to get our picture taken in the sticker photo booth. And we have room for a fourth face. So you can come." And Harmony told me she smiled really nicely and said, "Thanks, but no thanks."

Not even "Oh geez, I can't because I have to babysit/I'm grounded/I'm allergic to the ink they put on those photo strips." Just "Thanks, but no thanks." Sawyer and the Jennifers were totally stunned. Sawyer Sullivan rejected?! Sawyer gave her a look to kill and that was the end of that. Harmony is now a sore spot with Sawyer. And I am, too—guilty by association.

But I'm not Harmony. And I couldn't get a White Bubble going no matter how hard I tried. My face was bright red.

"Sawyer is pure Evil," Lindsay whispered, to make me feel better.

"White bubble, Jamie," Harmony commanded. "Stop worrying about what she thinks."

I knew I shouldn't let Sawyer get to me. But she did. Not just her nasty comments. But the way she looked at me. Like I was a nobody.

I have to confess. There's a little part of me that wants to be popular. Yes! It's better to have true friends than to be popular! I know, I know. But I also know, deep down, that if Sawyer had asked me to be the fourth face in her photo booth in seventh grade . . . I would have said yes.

I looked across the cafeteria. My sister was sitting over there with her new boyfriend, Duh. OK, his real name was Doug, but trust me, "Duh" worked.

I know all about being popular, vicariously, through her.

Allie is Popular. She was voted Fall Homecoming Princess of the Junior Class, which puts her in line for the pinnacle of junior popularity: Prom Princess. I see the benefits. Your choice of guys. People wanting to be your friend. When you're popular, you don't have to worry about what anyone thinks of you. Because you know they think you're cool, right?

Anyway, if I were IS, I wouldn't worry what Sawyer thought of me. I'd just Flick her away. He he. Thinking of Flicking Sawyer made me smile for a second.

"So what *did* you write your essay about, Jamie?" Lindsay asked me. "It must be great."

Well, that whole thing was really weird. Gallagher isn't one of those Read-Aloud types. A Do-Over type, yes. A See-Me type, definitely. But not a Read-Aloud type. Huh. Maybe my ploy of writing about Gallagher's studmuffin's subject worked even better than I'd hoped. Or Gallagher was seriously into good posture. I racked my brain for anything extra humiliating I might have put in my paper. Did I delete the part about a backpack that was too heavy getting caught in your bra strap? OMG. Marco Vega is in Gallagher's class with me. I am going to die. I am so going to die.

~

IS knew that she had to move fast. She had to destroy Myrna's Clique, before they crushed every girl's spirit.

4

"You aren't going to die, Miss Bartlett. You have no fever. You may return to class." Ms. Wingley, School Nurse, offered no help. Hopes for lying on the cot with a thermometer in my mouth for seventh-period English were in vain. I would have to stay strong.

"Hey, Jamie." Malik Green was on his way into Gallagher's. Connor Griffith, the kind-of-new guy, was walking with him. I've known Malik since first grade, so I'm pretty immune to him. I didn't know Connor too well, since he was new last year. I'd heard he was going out with one of the Jennifers.

"Word's your essay is going to be read out loud today," Malik said. "Hope you don't put us to sleep."

Thanks, Malik. *So* not helpful.

"I think it's just a rumor Sawyer Sullivan started to torture me," I said quickly. "And it's working."

"Well if it's true, it's pretty cool," said Connor. "Gallagher used to work at some publishing job in the city. If she's going to read it to everyone, it's got to be good."

"No, what I wrote is really stupid," I said. "You don't have to take pity on me."

"How about just saying 'Thank-you-Connor-for-saying-that-my-essay-has-got-to-be-good?'" Connor said to me.

I looked away. I always feel stupid when someone compliments me. Especially a guy. Not that it happens much.

"Um, yeah," I mumbled, and practically ran into the class-room.

We had assigned seats in Gallagher's class, and I slid into mine. *B* for Bartlett, right up front. Definitely a disadvantage in life, having an early letter for your last name. You have to give your answer first when teachers call on you alphabetically. You don't get to hear everyone else's answer and match it. So like if the teacher asks, "What did you think of the political debate last night?" And you answer, "I thought it was kinda interesting when they talked about education." And then the person behind you goes, "I dunno. I didn't watch it." And the next kid goes, "What debate?" And Sawyer Sullivan says, "I missed it, I was on a date." And of course you've now made yourself look like a total idiot.

Gallagher did a grammar lesson. Yawn. Then she went over all the stuff we're supposed to know for our test. Just when I thought maybe Sawyer had been trying to freak me out, Gallagher said that she wanted to read someone's essay out loud. I braced myself. She said it was about a girl who could change the world. Whew, she was starting with some-one else's essay. That's good, takes the focus off of just *moi*.

I tuned out Gallagher's voice and killed time by peeking at

Marco Vega. As a V, he's on the other side of the room but he's also toward the front. So he's still in viewing position if I kind of turn my seat and lean backward a little bit.

". . . And it was going around on the Internet that if Barbie were a real person, she wouldn't be able to physically hold her head up on that little body," Gallagher was saying. That was weird, I wrote about that in my journal last night. Someone else must have read that on the Internet, too, and put it in their essay. I wondered who it was.

Gross. I just got gum on my jeans. It must have been stuck to the bottom of the desk. I was scraping it off as I tuned back in to Gallagher. "The girl stuck a Post-it note on her mirror, just like Isabella told her. The Post-it note said, I'M ALL-OVER GORGEOUS."

OK, huh? Did Gallagher just say Isabella? Process, process . . . What are the chances that someone else wrote an essay about an Isabella and Post-it notes *and* quoted that thing about Barbie on the Internet?

Gallagher was talking about IS now. And Myrna. And Flicking.

It's true. Gallagher was reading my journal. Yes, she was, she was reading what I wrote for my very own self last night OUT LOUD to my entire English class. My private, personal journal is being announced to the universe. OMG OMG OMG.

Dizzy . . . dizzy . . . dizzy . . . feeling very dizzy. Get a grip, Jamie. OK. How did this happen?! I must have attached the wrong document to my email. I sent my journal to Harmony and she printed that out instead of my English paper.

I am such an IDIOT!

"And then IS said, 'It's time. It's time for things to change,'" Miss Gallagher was going on. And on. And on. This is bad. Way, way bad.

I sneaked a look around. Most importantly: Marco Vega. Marco was spacing out, tying and retying his shoelaces. OK, maybe this was no big deal. No one ever pays attention in class, right? I calmly turned around to peek at the rest of the class.

No one was even looking at me. They were all looking at Gallagher. Harmony. Malik. Connor. One of the Jennifers. Even Sawyer Sullivan. Oh no. Nobody was looking at me because they were so embarrassed for me. This was my journal! IS changing the world, beating Myrna and kicking Popular Butt.

Oh no. Myrna.

I took an extra peek at Sawyer and noticed that her eyes were looking squinty and meaner than usual. Yup, I was in trouble.

White bubble, white bubble. I pretended I was Harmony. OK. Worse-case scenario, I'm laughed out of Whittaker High. There are other schools—I could transfer, right? Foreign exchange program? In a country far, far away? I could handle this. White bubble, white bubble. Oh, why did I have to write such a long journal entry? This was taking forever. Finally, Gallagher said, "The End."

It was totally silent for, like, an eternity. I tried to sneak another look to see if everyone was asleep. It was the weirdest thing. Everybody was staring at me. People looked shocked or like they had been punched in the stomach. Rebecca Ferman looked like she was going to cry. I tried to look at Harmony but she was sitting in the *P*'s, so I couldn't see her. I felt eyes burning into me. I did notice Marco Vega totally asleep on his desk. Well, at least he didn't witness my humiliation.

Finally, Gallagher spoke.

"Any comments?"

For a moment nobody spoke. Then I heard Sawyer's voice. "I don't think this Isabella is very realistic," she said. "I mean no one thinks like that."

Then the bell rang. Saved! I heard Gallagher calling out my name, but I pretended I didn't hear her. My face was flaming hot. I fled from the room as fast as I could. Well, as fast as someone who trips over her backpack could.

~

I started walking down the hallway really quickly. I mean, it was just a journal entry, right? I hadn't even mentioned the word "bra" or anything. Then I thought about everyone staring at me, and my face went all hot again.

"Jamie! Wait up!" Harmony came running up to me.

"Harmony! That was *so* not my paper for English! That was my journal! You printed out my journal!"

"Are you serious?" Harmony said. "That was your journal? Not your homework?"

"I can't believe this," I wailed. "I guess I attached the wrong document to my email. I'm just so totally humiliated!"

"Totally what? Humiliated? What are you talking about?" Harmony said. "Gallagher wants to see you! You have to go back and talk to Gallagher!"

Harmony dragged me back toward the English room. Well, I thought, at least everyone would be gone by then.

Or not. A bunch of people were standing around Gallagher's desk. They all looked at me.

"Jamie, I'd like to talk to you," Gallagher said. "Everyone else, please move along to your next class."

"Harmony, don't go," I whispered to her. I needed moral support.

Everybody started to leave. Then the weirdest thing happened. As Clover McKay walked by me, she raised her fist: Flick! Flick! She was doing IS's hand flicking at me! Oh great, I thought. Even the class outcast is making fun of me.

Gallagher was sitting on her desk and started to tell me that she had never seen anything like the reaction that occurred after she read my essay. That everyone was deeply affected by it. That I ran out of the classroom before I heard what anyone else had to say. Gallagher told me that half the class had stayed to beg for a copy of my essay.

"You mean they *liked* what I wrote?" I squeaked.

"*Liked it?!*" Harmony exploded. "Jamie, what you wrote was unbelievable. Everybody was stunned."

"But Sawyer said—" I interrupted.

"Oh, come on—Sawyer Sullivan? *She* wouldn't get it. It's the Sawyer Bitches of the World that IS was conquering. Oops, sorry, Miss Gallagher," Harmony added.

"I think we are all a bit overcome with emotion after hearing what Jamie wrote," Gallagher said. "However, let's try to be more respectful of our fellow students in the future, shall we? Now I'd like to have a word with Jamie. So excuse us, Harmony, if you will."

~

"So Gallagher goes on and on about my journal entry and about IS," I told Lindsay later. Lindsay had said she heard all these people talking about me in the halls, and she wanted to know what was going on. Since it's not like people usually talk about me at school. Like never.

"First Gallagher asked if she could make copies for everybody in the class," I said. "I'm like, uh, whatever, I guess so. Then she tells me she has a friend who is a literary agent in Manhattan. Gallagher asked if she could fax her my story," I told her.

"What's a literary agent?" Lindsay asked.

"I have no idea." I shrugged. "I better get to Spanish."

I got to Spanish late and slid into my seat. As soon as I walked in, everyone was quiet. Kelly Hogan held something up and waved it at me, smiling. It was a copy of my journal entry! That was weird. She wasn't even in my English class.

All of a sudden, Rebecca Ferman held her hand up and

started flicking. And then maybe ten people were in there going *Flick, Flick, Flick.*

Señora Goldstein came in and started class. I couldn't pay attention. I was still trying to figure everything out. I'd never been more confused in my life. Gallagher was all excited about my story. Harmony was all excited about my story. People were flicking at me. Señora Goldstein even stopped talking in Spanish for one second so that we could understand her for a change: "Would the *chicos* and *chicas* who are doing that flicking thing with their hands please control themselves until after class? *Gracias.*"

A note slid under my foot. I picked it up and read it. *Tu cuento es bueno.* "Your story is good." I turned around and saw Connor Griffith giving me the thumbs-up. I rolled my eyes, but I was kind of starting to smile. Maybe this wasn't the worst thing that ever happened to me. OK, I would be a little bit of a celebrity with my English class today. Then it would wear off, and things would go back to normal.

IS found the first Villainess from the Evil Clique of Populars at cheerleading tryouts.

"Nice haircut," The Insultor was saying to a girl who was trying out. "Your mom put a bowl over your head?" She laughed and started to toss off another putdown. "Nice zit—" But IS raised her hand. The Insultor gasped. FLICK! IS put her down. On the floor. Permanently.

Harmony and I were in the gym after school. Watching the Pom Squad tryouts. NOT that I wanted to. Seriously, I have nothing against cheerleading. If I was even slightly coordinated I secretly think I'd make a fun cheerleader. I could cheer on Marco Vega!

> *Marco! Marco! He's my man!*
> *If he can't do it, no one can!*

Although Marco isn't a football player. He is cooler than even the football players. In the hierarchy of Whittaker freshman guys, it goes Marco first, *then* the football players, then the basketball players, and so on down.

Anyway. I've heard at some schools cheerleaders are perfectly nice, fun, great girls. But not at Whittaker.

I have a theory. At Whittaker, all the cheerleaders use up their smiling and cheeriness at the games. Then when they go off the field, they have none left.

Like my sister, Allie. Allie's a junior, co-captain of the squad, and one of the judges of the Poms. So she and all her snotty friends vote in other snotty girls like themselves. It's a vicious cycle.

Sawyer Sullivan was about to try out for one of the freshman spots on JV. Of course we all knew she was going to make it, but she had to go through the formality of trying out.

The Pom tryouts did have a huge element of suspense going for them. See, there were only *two* freshman spots available on JV. So if Sawyer got one of them and one of her Jennifers got another . . . then what would happen to the leftover Jennifer? This could be a crisis.

I didn't want to be there in case Sawyer spotted me. But Harmony's a reporter for the school newspaper, and her assignment was to write an article on Pom tryouts, so she had talked me into going to tryouts with her. I owed her for, oh, a zillion things she's done for me so I had to go. But also part of me was hoping there would be like some huge shifting of the universe. Like Mackenzie Watson, who won junior state gymnastics, would get a spot. But she'd recently joked about the pajamas Sawyer had worn at a sleepover back in third grade, so she was currently on the Populars' blacklist.

Sawyer was on the other end of the gym with the Jennifers, practicing her jumps. All of a sudden she turned and saw me. She said something to her Jennifers, and they started walking over.

"Uh-oh," I said to Harmony. "This can't be good. You don't think Sawyer knows that the Myrna character was based, um, *loosely* based of course, on her, do you?"

"Nah," Harmony said. "She's too dumb to figure that out."

But Sawyer and her Jennifers were definitely heading our way. And they did not look happy. They marched over to where Harmony and I were sitting. The Jennifers wore matching T-shirts and little shorts. Sawyer was all out in her gold and brown hair ribbons, T-shirt, and shorts with her *Whittaker High Rocks!* socks from the Varsity Pom Squad's fund-raiser for underprivileged cats.

"Then again," Harmony added, "Jennifer2 is kind of smart. She might have figured it out *for* Sawyer."

UH-OH.

"Hi, Sawyer," I squeaked brightly. "Hi, Jennifer. Hi, Jennifer."

"Jamie Bartlett," Sawyer said casually, "for some reason people seem to think the villain in your English essay—that Myrna character—sounds a little like me."

"But how can that be? Myrna is such a bitch," Harmony said, all innocent.

"Because Myrna has long blonde hair with two teeny braids in it and a perfect body and teeth," said Jennifer1 platinum hair (as opposed to Jennifer2 brown hair). "And she was trying out for Poms *and* she wore Pooh pajamas to a third-grade sleepover party."

"That's enough," Sawyer snapped. "I'm serious, Jamie Bart-lett." She shoved her little Sawyerface real close to me. "I better not hear another word about this Myrna character again or you are in deep—"

"All freshman girls on the floor!" barked the JV cheerleader co-captain, aka my sister, Allie. Whew, for once I was grateful for Allie's big mouth. Sawyer glared at me, then put on a big fake smile as she and the Jennifers pranced to the gym floor.

"I am so out of here. NOW," I said to Harmony. Being the true BFF she was, she came with me to hide out until the late buses arrived.

~

"I can't stop thinking about IS," Harmony said. "I didn't know you had it in you. I mean, all of my years of indoctrination are working. You're finally getting some backbone."

"Me? That would be nice," I said. "I mean, it's not like I'm Isabella. In my fantasies, in my dreams, I'm Isabella. In real life, I'm living in fear of a PsychoPom."

Yeah, wouldn't that be nice if the Flick really worked? Allie? *Flick!* Sawyer? *Flick!* Too bad it was just something I journaled.

Ugh. And there was the PsychoPom now.

Sawyer and Marco were walking out of school together. He was running his hands through her perfect hair. Oops, she didn't like him messing up her hair, and she pushed him away a little bit. They started making out.

"Quick, our bus is here! Let's go!" I said to Harmony, and started walking really fast with my face down. Don't look up, Sawyer, don't look up. Keep kissing, keep kissing. Sawyer lived on the other side of town. She took a different bus. There's no need for her to look this way.

"Hey, isn't that the Isabella girl?" someone yelled from the bus window.

"Jamie! Jamie! Over here!" someone else shouted. "IS! IS! IS!"

All of a sudden, a bunch of fists started coming out of the bus windows. *Flick! Flick! Flick!* There was flicking everywhere.

"You've been spotted," Harmony said, and pointed.

Uh-oh. Sawyer Sullivan had looked up. And her eyes squinted when she saw me.

"RUN!" I yelled to Harmony, and we made a break for our bus.

"I never even heard of Jamie Bartlett before," I heard someone saying as I jumped on the bus. I lost Harmony and shoved myself into one of the few empty seats. Whew. Made it past Sawyer.

I sat down next to some kid I didn't know. He pulled out some Xeroxed papers from his backpack and held them up.

"Hey, that was a cool story you wrote," he said. "I did something cool today, too." He reached into his backpack and pulled out a soggy paper towel. "I stole the dissected frog from biology today. Wanna see?"

I was online in our family room. Harmony and I were Instant Messaging.

WhyteBubble: u ran faster than IS today getting 2 that bus!

JustMe526: lol! If i were IS i would have just flicked ss away! Flick! cu later! 2 bad i am just me who runs away!

WhyteBubble: We need 2 work on that. EVERY1 is reading yr story. Lindsay sez it made her cry!

JustMe526: Oh shut up. What ru doing 2nite?

WhyteBubble: Helping Kameelah. She's having a hard time learning 2 read.

Harmony has a little half sister, Kameelah. She's so cute. If only I could trade her for Allie.

"Jamie, your English teacher is on the phone!" my mom was yelling to me from the kitchen. "Please come in the kitchen, *now.*"

I signed off and went into the kitchen. Yes, yes, into the *kitchen* to get the phone. No I don't have a phone in my room. Neither does Allie, ha-ha, which is about the worst thing that ever happened to her in her lifetime. And you aren't going to believe this: We don't even have a cordless phone. My parents are total dinosaurs. We have to stand there attached to a cord in the kitchen to talk to anyone. You can see how this could be tons of fun. Allie's new boyfriend even offered her his cell so she could hide out in her room. Mom said Nope.

Thank the lord for Internet access.

My mom was standing in our kitchen giving me *a look*. Like, it must be trouble if your English teacher is on the phone. Allie was coming out of the refrigerator with her usual diet soda can. She plopped down and put her plat-formed heels up on the kitchen table. I seriously don't know how she walks in those things.

"Oooh, Precious is in trouble," she sang. "This should be entertaining." I glared at Allie, but she just flipped me the finger. Mom can't see through Allie's 'I'm so Katie Holmes' cutie-pie façade, so the finger thing went right past her.

That pretty much sums up me and Allie. I give her dirty looks, and she gives me the finger back. It wasn't always like that. We used to actually hang out when we were kids. Playing Barbies and Polly Pockets. We almost never fought. When we did, we had a secret code word: RETSIS. Sister backward. That meant no matter what we were fighting about, we would stop and make up. OK, yeah, that's goofy.

But also, it was nice.

Then, all of a sudden, she totally changed. Her new friends came over and said things like, *Get out, Dork*. And then Allie started saying them, too. On better days, she ignored me completely. On bad days, she made fun of me, got me in trouble, and laughed about me to her friends. They were the Sawyer Sullivans of the Junior Class.

Ugh.

I looked at Mom, who was talking to Gallagher.

"She *what?*" My mom was practically shrieking.

Allie made finger slices-across-her-neck motions, like *You are so screwed*.

Uh-oh. Me in trouble? What did I do?

"Well, I can't believe it. Our Jamie?" Mom said. "I'm so *proud* of her."

Oh, Gallagher must be telling her about my essay. I stuck my tongue out at Allie, and oh great, of course Mom saw *that*.

Mom hung up the phone and sat down at the table. Here goes. I waited for the "no sticking out your tongue at your sister" lecture.

"Jamie, did you write a story for English class about a girl named Isabella who changes the world?" Mom asked me. Allie smiled, waiting for the punch line.

"Yeah, well kind of. I mean I wasn't writing it for English class, it was supposed to be for my journal. But Harmony gave me her laptop—and it's so much better for me to type on a laptop, oh Mom, it's so much more comfortable. We really should get one instead of the old computer we have—"

Mom interrupted. "Miss Gallagher wants to know if the writing is really yours. I mean, did you happen to take the idea from somewhere else?"

Oh, so *that's* it. Gallagher thinks I plagiarized. Allie got the drift even in her own dim way and was leaning back in her chair, smirking. I wondered if I could kick the back legs of her chair out without Mom catching me. *Bam!*

"Yes, Mom. I really wrote it. I swear. I didn't steal it from a book or from the Internet or buy it off Tyler Jones," I told her. Allie shot me a look. Tyler Jones is notorious for selling used research papers from the Net. Well, notorious with the students anyway. The parents don't know about him.

"I know, Jamie. I trust you. This is big news." Mom was suddenly smiling. "Miss Gallagher thought your paper was so good she faxed it over to her friend, who is a literary agent in New York. And, Jamie, the agent is interested in representing you."

Which led Allie, whose mood had dramatically changed, to ask, "What's a literary agent?" So Mom explained to both of us that a literary agent is a person who can help you get published and handle things for you. Like, say you wrote something you think is good enough to be a book. Instead of sending it directly to a publishing company, where they might be getting a zillion other submissions and don't have time to go through them all, you send it to a literary agent. If she likes it enough, she will sign you up as a client. And then use her connections to get editors interested. And then you might get published.

"Now, that doesn't mean you *will* get published," Mom said. "It's very, very difficult to get a book published these days." Yeah, Mom knows these things. Mom thinks about writing a book sometimes. She writes a column in the local newspaper. She gives advice about gardening questions, like what to do if a swarm of insects attacks your tomato plants. When her first column was published, we had a cake to celebrate. Yum. Maybe I'd get a cake.

"But I must say I'm impressed," Mom said. Allie got up and stomped off to her room.

"What, no congratulations? No huggy, no kissy for your little sister?" I called after her, making smoochy noises. He-he. Take that, Prom Princess.

Mom went to call Dad at work, and I was all happy because I could really use an A. I had two warnings in gym. So my continued inability to move properly could create a problem in my report card. I mean, having a gym-class grade count the same as biology just isn't right. Injustice.

If you're wondering why I didn't jump up and down all over with excitement, well, come on. I'm a pretty realistic person. It's not like I thought anything more would happen. That anything had happened in the first place was pretty out there. I would just be secretly pleased that things had gotten this far and that people liked my journal entry.

I mean, what more could happen to me—normal, old, regular Jamie Bartlett?

**Q: Would you take off your clothes
and run around the school in your underwear
for $1,000? $3,000? $5,000?**

Harmony, Malik, Connor, and I were sitting in the back of study hall first period. We were obviously studying hard. Harmony wasn't even in my study hall. But she had a sub in French, and I had a sub in study hall, so she sneaked in for a visit.

Harmony skipped a lot of classes. I was always nervous she'd get caught. But she said teachers were never sure if she was supposed to be here or in the city and nobody kept track. And she says she's an individualist who feels constricted by the artificial and seemingly arbitrary rules the school bureaucracy imposes anyway. (Plus, it's not like her mother really cares, so why should she be bored?)

Anyway, she's here in study hall.

Malik had asked the question.

Malik said he would do it for 100 bucks. And that he would pay Harmony $5,000 if *she* would run around the school in her underwear. Harmony Flicked him.

Connor asked if he did it, could it be after school, outside but not on a day when the cheerleaders were out there practicing?

Things had calmed down at school. I mean, I'd gotten Flicks from people in the halls over the past week and a half. But it was pretty much back to normal for me. I did talk to my agent, Leslie, on the phone. She seemed really nice. Leslie talked to me and my parents about stuff that probably wouldn't happen anyway, like signing a contract and being interviewed by newspaper people.

Harmony had done a bunch of online research for me about book publishing. She emailed me what she found out. Be patient, she advised. When a literary agent accepts you as a client, it takes time. She has to try to find the right publisher to publish the manuscript. Then if someone *does* buy it, there will be negotiations and paperwork. OK by me—I had other things to think about that were more likely to come true in my lifetime, like someone offering me thousands of dollars to run around school in my underwear.

"Well, Jamie?" Malik asked. "One thousand bucks . . . would you do it? Three thousand? Five thousand . . . going, going, gone."

I said no, no, no—thinking of my training-bra situation. Not even for $5,000.

"And the reason is . . . ," Malik asked.

"Can we change the subject," I mumbled. In front of Malik, the underwear topic was not so much a big deal. But Connor and underwear . . . OK, I was blushing on that one. Connor is kind of cute. Better than average. Brown hair, brown eyes. Not tall, not short. And he has this way of looking right in your eyes when he talks to you. I blushed harder.

"Yeah, I'll change the subject," said Connor. He was looking at his pager, checking sports scores. "Jamie, your real name doesn't happen to be Jameson, does it?"

Everyone looked at me. I mean, I was pretty much Jamie everywhere; even on roll call. I mean, Jameson is such a guy's name. James King, well she can get away with it—I mean, look at her. If I called myself Jameson, with my chest, people would think I really was a guy.

"Um, yeah, on my birth certificate," I started to say. Connor just handed me his pager. I watched the little electronic letters scroll across the Entertainment News.

High school freshman's manuscript sells to Parker Press following a frenzied bidding war. According to a Parker spokesperson, the manuscript by Whittaker High School student Jameson Bartlett will be the lead title on its forthcoming list. . . .

I dropped the pager on the desk.
Buzzing, my head is buzzing. . . .

"I think she's going to pass out!" I vaguely heard Malik say. "Stand back, everybody!"

"Jamie, breathe!" Harmony said.

"Put your head on the desk," said Connor.

Breathe. Breathe. Book. Sold. Lead. Title. Jameson. Bartlett. Me. Breathe.

"Principal Litagaki wants to see Jamie Bartlett in his office," another voice said.

"I think you better walk her down there," Connor told Harmony, smiling. "She might even need to be carried."

So, yes, well. That was how I found out that I was about to be a published author. I got more details in the principal's office. Principal Litagaki and Miss Gallagher were in the office, jumping up and down. No, seriously, you never would have known it was a principal and an English teacher. They looked like they were trying out for Poms.

They gave me the scoop. The agent had sent my story to some big publishing companies. They got all excited over it. They had an instant bidding war, which is what happens when more than one publisher wants to buy your book. So there I was in school all day, worrying about gym, not knowing I was involved in some publishing battle. I felt kind of like Helen of Troy.

Un. Be. Lievable.

And they told me how much money was involved. And it was not a tiny amount of money, either. Like if they offered me $5,000 to run around the school in my underwear, I could just laugh—ha-ha-ha—$5,000, no way.

I WAS ABOUT TO BE RICH!!!!

$$$$$$$! $$$$$$$! $$$$$$$!

$$$$$$$$$$$$$$$$$$$$$$$$!

8

Not that the money was going to make any difference in my immediate life, thank you very much Mr. and Mrs. Over-Protective Bartlett. Later that night we were sitting around the dining-room table. Mom had broken out her fancy plates and silverware on account of me being an almost-published author.

"How about a new laptop? That would help my writing career," I suggested. So far the parents had vetoed a new house with my own bathroom, an apartment in the city like Harmony's, and the Maserati Spyder I had heard Marco Vega talking about in English class once. Not that I could drive it for a couple years. But it would look cool.

But noooo, said the 'rents. No house, no bathroom, no apartment, no Spyder, not even a laptop. I was beginning to see a pattern here.

"We don't want all this to change our lives too much," my parents said. Over and over again.

"OK, a phone. A simple measly cell phone. Or a phone in my room. At least a *cordless* phone based in the kitchen?!"

I tried. What good was this bonanza if I couldn't even get a phone out of it?

"Jamie, the money will be put into a college fund for you. And the remainder will be given to you in trust when you are older," Dad explained. "Much older."

"But don't I get to see just a little teeny bit of it?" I wailed. "I mean, come on. I sold a book."

"Jamie, we are incredibly proud of you," my dad said. "But we want to be responsible with the financial aspect of it. We are comfortable now, and your money is better off put away."

"Although, Steven, we could use a new dishwasher . . . ," Mom said.

"Do I still have to load it?" I asked.

"YES," my parents said, in stereo. Geez. If I couldn't have money, couldn't I at least get out of my chores?

"Maybe we can take a nice family vacation to celebrate when things die down a bit," Dad said. "Maybe Gettysburg, Pennsylvania, to learn more about the Civil War."

Oh, swell.

Guess Mom agreed with me about Gettysburg.

"Maybe the ocean," she whispered to me. And then she spoke up. "But I have a nice surprise for you in the meantime, Jamie. We're going shopping tonight."

"Shopping?" Allie perked up at that one.

"Yes," Mom said. "We need to get Jamie an outfit. My newspaper wants to interview her tomorrow after school."

"What about me?" Allie whined. "Next Thursday is school spirit day when we all wear our cheerleader uniforms. And I could use a new outfit to wear to school on Wednesday—the day before when everyone is looking at me."

Oh, in case you are dying of suspense, here are the cheerleading results. Sawyer made the Pom Squad. You are so surprised, right? And Jennifer1, with the platinum hair. Jennifer2 was chosen as one of the substitutes and was last seen in the girls' bathroom crying, with her new best-friend-by-default-fellow-pom-reject Mackenzie Watson consoling her.

"Allie, your mom and Jamie are going to have a special mother-daughter night tonight," my dad was saying to my sister. "But I have a little surprise treat for you, too. I got the new guidebook to colleges! We can read it together! It's never too early to plan, Allie."

9

"Your belt is SO last season," the Fashionistor sneered. "And your jacket? Can you say Discount Store?" But then she gasped. IS had appeared!

The Fashionistor tried to escape, but this season's must-have heels were so high she couldn't run in them. The Fashionistor exploded in a burst of fabric.

I tried to go to sleep. I was tired. Shopping with my mom can be exhausting. I was all worried about what to wear that would look cool. I even tried to think, WWSW? (What would Sawyer wear?), but my mom NO'd everything as too expensive. Or not appropriate. I even had started to wish that Allie had come along; at least she had fashion sense.

I finally talked Mom into this sweater and skirt, kind of like the one Jennifer1 had worn the other day. The skirt was a little short so I had to keep pulling the waistband down. The sweater was kind of itchy. But I would look good for the interview.

Ack! I WAS GOING TO BE INTERVIEWED FOR THE NEWSPAPER.

Only one slightly major thing here. I mean, I was not known as a good talker. It would never be Regis and Jamie. What was I going to say?! What if I said something stupid, and everyone read it and laughed at me?! Who am I trying to kid? When do I NOT say something stupid? So I was up all night feeling really nauseous.

Here I was, about to be a published author and apparently in the newspaper and on TV. No Maserati, no phone, no raise in my allowance. And now, potential humiliation in the media. And people want to be famous authors because . . . *why?!?*

~

Joe, the reporter for the newspaper, said he'd just ask a few questions. He assured me it would be easy and painless. We sat in the kitchen, with Mom nearby. In case Joe asked me something shocking, I guess.

"How do you feel now that you're about to become an author, Jamie?" Joe asked me.

"It still doesn't seem real," I told him.

"And tell me how you came to write a book?"

I told him about the assignment for Gallagher's class and how I came up with Isabella. I left out the obsession with Amber Tiffany. And any mention of Sawyer.

The photographer started taking pictures. "Pretend I'm not here," she said. "I want totally natural shots."

Joe asked me more questions.

"If you could, please try to stay a little more still," the photographer said.

"Sorry, I'll try," I told her, squirming around. My sweater was itching like crazy.

"That's OK. I'll try a different angle where it won't matter so much," the photographer said.

She got down on the floor and started shooting from there.

"Did you base your characters on real people?" Joe asked me.

"NO! Absolutely not!" I thought of Sawyer. Maybe that would help squash that, uh, entirely untrue rumor. "You can say that no character is, um, fully based on anyone I know."

He asked more questions—nothing too hard—and then he said, "Well, that wraps things up. It was a pleasure meeting such a nice young lady, and I look forward to hearing great things about your success."

"See? That wasn't so bad," Mom said after Joe and the photographer left. "You did a nice job."

Yeah, that wasn't too bad. Uncomfortable. Not exactly fun. But I didn't say anything stupid. So, OK. Whew.

I ran upstairs and ripped off my new outfit and put on something comfortable. Ah. It was over!

~

Local Teen About to
Become Published Author

"It still doesn't seem real," says Jamie Bartlett.

~

"Here's the newspaper, Judy Blume," Allie purred as I came down the stairs the next morning. She was sitting at the kitchen table, chugging her healthy diet-soda breakfast.

"Now, Allie," Dad said. "It's a lovely article about Jamie, and we are very proud of her." Why did Dad sound like he was warning her?

"Oh it's not the article that's bad," Allie said, shoving the newspaper at me. "There you are, glamour girl."

Wow, front page. A big article. An even bigger picture. Of basically my nostrils. OMG. There I was, one big face, and you could totally see up my nose. My Nostrils were the Page 1 News of the Day.

"How did the photographer even *get* that angle?" Allie asked, all innocent. "Did she lie on our floor and say, 'Let's see if I can get a close-up of Jamie's boogers.'?"

"It's a very *artistic* shot," contributed Mom brightly. "It has lovely . . . well . . . shadowing."

"That's it," I announced. "I'm so over being in the media. I won't be in newspapers, on television, on the radio. I won't be onstage or even appear in school today. What if anyone sees this?"

"Oh, it's a bee-yoo-tiful pinup poster," Allie said. "I bet Marco Vega is gazing at you over his cereal, thinking, 'What lovely snot she has.'"

"Shut up, Allie!" That's *it*, I *had* to get a phone in my room. I must have slipped up on my code name for Marco,

WFPJ (Whittaker's Freddie Prinze, Jr.). Allie was such an eavesdropping sneak.

No way was I showing my face in school today. Or ever. I actually thought I gave a semi-intelligent interview. But no one was going to read it. They would be scared off by the Giant Nostrils from Hell.

Doorbell. It was Harmony, holding a copy of the paper.

"Hi, Mr. Bartlett, Mrs. Bartlett, Allie. Hi, Celebrity."

"I can't go to school," I said. "Everyone will be staring at my nose." I lowered my voice so only Harmony could hear me. "Teach me how to skip."

"No way," Harmony whispered back. "Unlike mine, *your* parents would notice."

"Sweetie, you do have to go to school," Mom said. "You've got that math quiz." Harmony gave me a look like, see?

"OK, it's not the most flattering picture ever," Harmony admitted. "But I bet Sawyer Sullivan is still jealous. I mean, front page? Even *she* hasn't gotten that action. So come on, the bus is almost here." Harmony dragged me out the door to the bus stop.

"Have a nice day," Allie said sweetly. Her boyfriend of the week had a car, so no rushing to the bus for her. When I get my Maserati Spyder, she's *so* not going to be allowed even to sit in it.

Bidding War
Over Book by
Teen Author

In a move that is shaking up the book
industry, Parker Press has announced
that it has signed a manuscript written
by 14-year-old Jameson Bartlett in an
unprecedented bidding war.

"It's wise, it's funny—it's a book
we think all girls will love. And yes, it
really was written by a 14-year-old!"
said editor Denise Silver.

~

I have an editor at Parker Press, Denise. Her job is to take my
journal entry, which she calls a manuscript, and see that it
turns into a book. She works with my agent to get the contract done. She works with the designer to make the cover
and inside look nice. She works with me to make my words
work perfectly.

I had to do some more writing of the story so it would be

long enough to be a book. I got to skip a week of school and sit in my room and write, write, write. Perfect timing to hide out from Sawyer and let her simmer down. Harmony let me borrow her laptop, and I stared at Amber Tiffany on my wall. I got those feelings back and cranked. Finally Denise said, "You got it! It's done!"

Whew! I was exhausted. But it could have been worse.

"Usually, there would be many more revisions on your end," Denise told me over the phone. She probably realized I didn't know what that meant, so she explained. "Which means I would edit your book and ask you to make suggested changes. Most authors have to do many, many rounds of what you just did. But in your case, I'm trying to leave it pretty much untouched, since it rings so true in your own words."

"So it's like when Gallagher gives me a paper back and tells me to correct my mistakes and turn it in again?" I asked.

"Exactly! But this is as if Miss Gallagher is correcting your mistakes for you. And giving you an A-plus to boot," Denise said.

I was really liking Denise. She told me how this was a rush process because of all the excitement about my book. She called all the talk about my book "buzz." Because you were starting to hear stuff about my story on the radio and on the Internet. And seeing those headlines in the magazines like the one that said:

WHAT IS IS?

AND WHY THE WORLD WILL KNOW SOON . . .

And there were already five fan websites and about fifty *IS* Google links.

So anyway, usually it takes a year or more to get a book out in the bookstores. But to take advantage of the buzz, they were making it a rush book. So it would be out in like a couple of weeks.

A couple of weeks! OK, a lot of what has happened so far has been pretty, well, hideous and embarrassing. But let's move on. There would be a book out there with my name on it sitting on the bookshelf. And some girl might walk by and go, "Oh, this looks kind of interesting." And use her babysitting money to buy it. And read about IS, a character I made up in my very own head. And maybe, just maybe, she would like IS as much as I did. Wow. Wow.

~

Denise invited me to come to New York City and meet some "key players," as she called them. The good part was it was now one of Harmony's city months. Which usually sucked but meant this time that I could stay overnight with her at her mom's.

My new publisher sent a car to my house. A "limo service" my dad said, impressed. The driver asked me why I was going to the city. I told him "to meet my book publisher." He didn't believe it at first. Hey, I practically didn't believe it myself! I mean, I was about to meet my EDITOR and my AGENT. Up until now, it seemed a little unreal. More like a game. Sure, I was going to be an author. Yeah, right, I have an agent and an editor. It just didn't seem totally true.

I was petrified.

I mean, who am I to be having a book published? Jamie J. K. Rowling? Jamie Maya Angelou? Jamie Judy Blume? I'm not worthy of writing a book that will be on a shelf with *real* authors! There have got to be a ton of other talented teens who have more angst than me pouring their hearts onto paper! How did this happen to me?!

And now I was in a limo driving to Manhattan. It was really starting to sink in.

~

Which house is cooler:

A. A house in suburbia where the younger daughter is forced to share a bathroom with her nasty older sister

B. A huge apartment in Manhattan over-looking Central Park—and the girl who

lives there has one and a half bath-
rooms just for herself

Oh, it is *so* B. And I was sitting in B, in Harmony's room
eating dinner. We were sharing a chicken barbecue pizza,
and she was grilling me about my day.

"They got you a limo, huh? Stretch or regular?" she asked.

"Regular. I guess more like a big car. But still cushy. And
Leslie and Denise took me to this restaurant," I told her.
"The review on the wall said it was a five star. I had crispy
salmon." I tried to sound blasé—oh yeah, I did this all the
time.

"Swanky!" said Harmony. "Just think, you could have
been eating meat loaf surprise back at Whittaker today."

Yeah, I just wish I could have enjoyed it more. But I had
been a TOTAL WRECK. Fortunately, Leslie and Denise
were *sooo* nice. Leslie told me about her daughter, Gabriela,
who was a freshman, too. After Leslie had first read my story,
she asked Gabriela to take a look. Gabriela totally loved
Isabella and told Leslie she had to sign me up as a client.

Even though they were nice, I couldn't relax. I mean, I was
supposed to be impressing them. Denise's company just spent
a lot of money for something that came out of my head. I
wanted to show her my head was worth it. But when they
asked me things about school and how I felt about everything, I was all nervous. I mean, what do I have to say to
them that would be even remotely interesting?

And they made me more nervous when they told me

what was coming. More publicity! More newspapers! Radio! *Television!*

"Harmony, I'm really freaking out. What if they take the contract back?" I worried out loud. "What if they thought I was an idiot?"

Because what if I was a disappointment? What if they were expecting . . . IS?

Isabella would have waltzed in and known just what to order. She would have told entertaining and intelligent stories.

I, on the other hand, had no idea what to order. Just copied what Leslie asked for. Dropped my fork on the floor and got sauce on my shirt. Got lost on the way back from the bathroom. Then crashed into a waiter. And said *Um* a lot.

"Jamie. For one day in your life, can you enjoy the moment? They liked your story," Harmony reassured me. "I'm sure they liked you."

"You think?" I really needed to hear it.

"I *know*," Harmony said firmly. "You are a worrier. And a terrible dancer. But you are totally likable. And if you don't start appreciating all of this, I'm going to have to go in your place. Because I would kill for some crispy salmon. Did they have gravlax? Yum. Although this pizza is pretty tasty."

"Yeah, the pizza is *sooo* good," I said, having no idea what gravlax was. "So is your room. So is your apartment. I mean, puh-leez. You can walk to everything. And the view? The park? The housekeeper? The stud-puppy doorman?"

"Yeah, Eduardo is pretty cute." Harmony sighed.

"I don't know how you can stand going back upstate," I said. "Aside from the fact that I'm there," I added quickly.

"Yeah, I love the city. But I do get really lonely," she said. "Up there I've got you, Lindsay, Kameelah. My dad. Beryl." Beryl was her stepmother. She was pretty nice.

"Well, you've got your mom down here," I reminded her.

"Yeah, right. I mean, let's see. It's eleven at night. And she's still at work. Like always. I used the money on the table for take-out. I got a note saying I have a hair appointment tomorrow and the cab fare is left for me. And Richard is always flying around the world on some deal. I see The Ogre more than I see them."

The Ogre is Harmony's governess. She comes from noon to four every day to do the Whittaker High curriculum with Harmony. Harmony says she's worse than any Whittaker teacher because she's so strict and serious. But I'd trade for the Ogre so I could sleep late and do school in four hours. Any day.

But Harmony hadn't made any real friends down here. Her mom had moved down here when she married Richard about a year ago, and Harmony hadn't really settled in. Harmony's mom had signed her up to see a therapist in the city when her parents first got divorced, to "help her adjust." That's when Harmony started skipping classes. The therapist told her the reason she was skipping was to get her mom's attention. Harmony ended up skipping therapy. Her mother didn't even notice that either.

"Leslie's daughter, Gabriela, sounds kind of cool," I said to Harmony. "I should hook you up with her. I'll ask Leslie."

~

We talked until midnight and went to bed. I couldn't sleep because I was worrying.

"Harmony? You awake?" I whispered.

"Mmmmph?" came from the other twin bed.

"Are you sure I can do this?"

"Yes. Go to sleep."

"Harmony?"

"What?

"Do you think I need a nose job?" I asked, thinking about the schnoz article.

Whomp! A stuffed frog flew across the room and hit me in the face.

"There's your nose job. Good NIGHT, Jamie."

I smiled and fell asleep.

11

"Your chest, Jamie, it's all about your chest," Diana said.

If it was all about my chest, I was in big, big trouble.

It was the next day, and first on the schedule was a meeting with my media coach.

You might remember her name from my *Mora Live!* appearance I was telling you about? She's the one who was supposed to help me look my best for all the author appearances I would be doing.

"You need to stick your chest out more, Jamie. Pull your shoulders back. Head up. There you go," Diana moved my body parts around until I was positioned to her satisfaction. It felt like I was about to fall over backward.

"Look at yourself in the mirror. See how much more confident you look?"

I looked. It felt weird, but it was true. I had to believe Diana on that one. She was seriously confident. She used to be a fashion model and she walked into the room like she was on a runway. With attitude. Diana was wearing a black pantsuit. Black bobbed hair. Spiky strappy heels. Little glasses on a chain around her neck that she used to peer at me close up.

"There will be no self-consciousness here, Jamie," were the first words Diana said to me. She had put her hands on my shoulders and stared right in my eyes. "No insecurity. We work together to bring out your best qualities. And make you shine in and out of the spotlight."

She had given me a sheet of paper. My name was at the top. A list said:

> Posture
> Gestures
> Voice
> Makeup
> Hair
> Clothing

"We'll cover all areas on this chart," Diana said.

"Hold it right there!" cried a voice from the corner. It was Harmony. She had called her governess and claimed she was too sick for tutoring. And she had talked Diana into letting her stay for the consultation, which took some pretty serious convincing. Diana said she wanted only the client, meaning me, in the room. So I would feel comfortable and have my privacy. But I wanted Harmony there, so we begged until Diana finally gave in.

"Excuse me." Harmony marched over to Diana. "But I see where this is going. You're going to try to change Jamie into someone she's not. Well, we like her *Before* and we don't need any *After*. You know that a message in her upcoming book is that you don't have to change yourself for *anyone!*"

Whoa. Go, Harmony. That sounded really good. But I was hoping Diana wasn't going to turn around and waltz out the door. I mean, good speech and all, Harmony, but hey. I wasn't *completely* happy with how I looked. For one thing, I was hoping maybe Diana would take me shopping for a Miracle Bra.

Diana smiled at Harmony in a softer way.

"Harmony, you are absolutely right. That does often happen in the entertainment business. Entertainers can be forced to conform to an image even when they aren't comfortable with it. And that's why Leslie and Denise chose me to work with Jamie. I help my clients to be more comfortable with themselves. I'll work with Jamie to bring out the best JAMIE she can possibly be. And help her not be nervous on camera," she added.

"I have one question for you," Harmony asked, still suspicious. "Have you ever coached Amber Tiffany?"

"Amber Tiffany?! Good lord, no. That girl is a walking plastic factory," Diana said.

"Oh." Harmony was mollified. "OK. Well, I'll go sit down now. But I'm watching you."

"Yes, I know you are," Diana said. "Now, Jamie. Let's get to work. Posture."

So we did these things to work on my posture. Like stretching. How to stand and walk confidently. It was kinda fun. And after a while even Harmony jumped up and did the exercises with me. Then Diana went out to the hallway to answer a call on her cell.

"Dahling, may I get you a spot of tea?" Harmony glided over to me, using her new posture and walking techniques.

"Not now, my pet, I'm in the midst of my fashion runway show." I moved down my imaginary catwalk.

"Wow, you didn't even trip," Harmony said admiringly. "So far this is OK. But I reserve judgment until makeup and hair time."

Later that afternoon, the driver said he'd drop Harmony at her apartment before taking me upstate. I read my cheat sheet out loud to Harmony.

Jamie's No-No List

1. Hold hands still, without playing with rings.
2. No nail picking. Or biting.
3. No squirming in my seat. Sit still.
4. Place feet flat on floor. Don't jiggle legs.
5. No slumping when I sit. Sit straight and let my body fill up the chair. Don't try to hide in a little ball. Take up space.
6. Don't chew on the inside of my cheek. Or my hair.

There were about twenty more JamieHabits to work on. Diana said I lose power when I do those things. Which is like all the time. She said if I get rid of these habits, I'll not only look more confident, I'll feel more confident.

"Like I will ever look confident," I said. "Ha!"

Harmony rolled her eyes.

"Harmony," I warned. "Don't forget your Rule Number One." Harmony's No-No list was a lot shorter than mine. Rolling her eyes was about her only bad habit. (Yeah, after a while Diana said what the heck and tossed in some free advice to Harmony.)

"Well, I'll see you soon." I hugged Harmony. And I would, yay! I had another appointment to come back to the city and work with Diana. Next up: "Talking to the Media." Not sure about that one. But then the next weekend, we would work on my appearance. Clothes! Hair! Makeup! How fun was that going to be?!?

"Size zero is the only way to be," the Dietor said scornfully. "Why, I'd be a negative number if I could!" The Dietor turned around to drink her diet soda and eat her single lettuce leaf. Then she gasped. IS! IS raised her fist and FLICK! the Dietor wasted away . . . to nothing.

~

I glided over to my locker. Chest out, shoulders back.

"Oh sorry," I said to the guy I bumped into.

I stuck a new Post-it note on the inside of my locker door, to remind me: Diana Rule #17: Watch where you're going.

Lindsay came over to my locker. When Harmony was in the city, I hung out with Lindsay more. I kind of felt guilty about Lindsay sometimes. When Harmony came back to town, Lindsay sometimes got stuck alone. Linds is great—she's so nice and so there for you. And we have fun when the three of us are together. But there are times I need it to be just H and me . . . we're always on the same wavelength.

"So I was thinking that maybe you could sleep over on Friday?" Lindsay was saying. "You can pick the videos. I could make those brownies you like, too. And I got a free sample of seaweed detox mask—we could split it . . ."

Rring, ring.

"Oh, it's my cell phone." I reached into my backpack. I loved saying that. Yes! My parents had finally given in and let me have a cell phone. Because things were really going on now that the book was about to be released. The cell phone was temporary until things died down, warned my parents. I was hoping they'd forget that last part.

Soon there would be an actual book! In the bookstores. In the grocery stores. On Amazon. At Target. At Wal-Mart. At Costco. Anywhere fine books are sold.

"Hello?" I said, answering the phone. It was Denise!

"Jamie! Where are you going to be in about a half hour?" she asked.

"Well, from one-oh-three to one-fifty-five I'm in English, room three-oh-six," I told her.

"Perfect," Denise said, and hung up.

"What was that all about?" Lindsay asked me.

I shrugged. "Don't know."

The warning bell rang.

"Well, I've got to go to health," Lindsay said. "The worst. Today is nutrition, chapter six. The Healthful Weight chapter."

Poor Lindsay. She was really hung up on her weight. Like who isn't. But it was really bumming Lindsay out. And her dad was definitely not helping. Once when I was over at her house, we were watching TV in the family room. And some girl comes onscreen and her father goes, "Whoa, get that porker off the screen." Lindsay turned beet red. I pretended I didn't hear him. But I was extra nice to her all night.

"Good luck in Health," I told her, and gave her shoulder a little squeeze.

I did my daily Marco Vega check as I sat down in English class. He was writing something and then folded it up into a note. I wondered what it said.

I wished it were a love poem. I wished he had written at the top: "At last! I can share my poetry with the one who really understands me." He would pass it over to Tirrell Nelson who would slide it to Priya Mahraza who would shoot it to Rebecca Ferman who would toss it on my desk . . . mine . . . mine!

But, as usual, I watched as Marco slid the note to Tirrell Nelson . . . who slid it to Sawyer Sullivan . . . who caught it under her little cheerleading sneakers with the gold and brown ribbons. Ugh.

I turned back fast before Sawyer caught me looking. I lived in fear of the day Sawyer decided to confront me about the whole Myrna thing. I'd been spending entire school days avoiding her. Fortunately she was so busy being the center of attention (Sawyer is a JV cheerleader! Bow down and worship her!) that I was able to stay under her radar.

Well, almost. Sawyer whispered something to Jennifer2.

They both looked at me and laughed. I shifted in my seat. I hate when they do that.

A knock on the door interrupted Gallagher's discussion of the new writing assignment. A guy in a delivery uniform came in and handed Gallagher a package. We waited while she signed for it.

"Jamie," she announced. "This is for you."

I'd never had a package delivered to me at school before. Actually I'd practically never had a package delivered to me *ever* aside from the ones from my great-grandmother. And those were usually frilly, pink dresses with smocks. Yes, I still got them, thank you. But my great-grandmother wouldn't send me anything at school, would she? Like a frilly, pink dress with a smock?

"Go ahead," said Gallagher. "Open it."

I tore off the packaging tape and peeked in the box. There were about ten books inside. Books with a purple cover. Books with *my* name on them.

"It's her book!" someone yelled. People crowded around my desk to see. I held up a copy.

"That's so cool!" Everyone was talking at once, congratulating me, all that. (Well, not *everyone*. Marco and Sawyer were taking advantage of the little break to make out on the radiator. But I was *not* going to let them spoil this moment.)

"What a great cover," Gallagher said. "It really pops!"

I turned my book over in my hands. I just stared at it.

"Hey, author," Connor said. "You must be psyched. Can I buy one of these copies off you? You'll have to sign it first."

My face was burning. He gave me a pen and smiled at me. I wrote, "To Connor, from Jamie Bartlett." Not very original. But hey—I was new at this. Plus people were sitting on my desk and talking about me. I was new at that, too.

"Hey, let me see that." The crowd parted. Like in slow motion, Marco Vega came over to my desk. Sawyer, I noticed, was still sitting on the radiator looking quite PO'd.

I handed a book to Marco.

"Whoa," he said. And he smiled. At me. OMG—he smiled at me.

"*IS* by Jameson Bartlett," Marco Vega said. "Dude. That's cool."

This was so seriously the moment I *knew*. This book really *was* going to change everything.

13

~

"So how does it feel now that your book is about to come out?" Harmony asked me. "On the record."

"Um, I don't know," I told Harmony. "I'll call you later."

"Come on, please? Just a couple of quotes. I'm trying to get this thing done for my deadline," Harmony said.

"Well, I left my folder at home," I told her. I had a folder of all the stuff Diana had taught me. I had made a page of answers I thought would be good for interviews. Kind of a cheat sheet.

"Jamie, you can answer my question without looking at your notebook, can't you?"

"Oh, OK. So you want to know how it feels? It feels great!

Exciting! Awesome!" I told her, thoughtfully. Harmony started typing. "And terrifying! And kinda embarrassing, like having to run around school in your underwear or something."

Wait. Did I just say underwear?

"Don't put that in there!" I shrieked. "Do not put that I said underwear in the school paper!"

"Calm down, don't freak out! I won't use that!" Harmony answered.

"See?" I groaned. "I DO need my cheat sheet. I always say something stupid!"

"Jamie." Harmony cut me off again. "This is only the school paper."

I know. And I could only imagine what was going to happen when the REAL interviews started.

~

"GirlZine, PreTween magazine, just look at all these websites . . ." My mom was reading a sheet of paper later that night at dinner. She held it out to my dad. "So, Jamie, you are supposed to do interviews when—after school? And when do they think you will do your schoolwork?"

I now had a publicist named Oliver who was starting to book me interviews. He wanted to start me off talking to people from websites, newspapers, and magazines. Radio and TV would come soon. Very soon, he said.

The books I'd gotten in school were a sneak preview, but

as of today everyone would be able to buy one. I mean, how cool is that? I would be able to go into any bookstore and wave toward a shelf. Oh yes, that's my book. I'd been practicing that wave in the mirror.

I was still really nervous about interviews. I mean, Harmony had to talk me into doing an interview just for the *school* paper.

"National media exposure would look good on Jamie's college application," Dad said to Mom. "Maybe we should rethink Jamie's school situation."

Maybe he meant telling my teachers to call off homework!

"Maybe we should pull you out of school," Dad said to me. "We could get you a tutor. I read about a tutor who specializes in gifted and talented writers."

"No!" I said. I mean, I used to be jealous of Harmony because of her whole "having a governess so she can sleep in" gig. But I didn't want to be pulled out of school right now because . . .

Marco Vega interaction! Ever since that moment when Marco smiled at me, things had changed. Now he said hi to me in the halls. He smiled at me in class. Marco Vega had finally noticed me!

We had a new bond, Marco and I. I mean, he was the guy who wrote that beautiful poem. And now he knew I was a writer just like he was. We have a connection. Two literary souls, destined for each other.

"I'm uh, really learning a lot in school right now to prepare me for college and all," I said. "I think I should stay in school."

"That's fine for now," Dad said. "But we'll reevaluate from time to time and see if things are getting to be too much."

"Well, maybe the media interviews would be good for Jamie's self-confidence." My mom was talking herself into it. "But I get to pull the plug at any time. Got it, Jamie?"

"Got it."

The next couple of days were major blur. I went to NYC to spend another day with Diana. Harmony couldn't come, though. She got caught for calling in sick to her governess. Beryl had called to check on something and Harmony had gotten snagged. Beryl told her *No more sick days*, and that was that. So Mom came with me to meet Diana.

The first part of Diana's session was how to act on radio, on TV, and for newspapers. Like how to talk as though you're really you and not try to be someone you aren't. Harmony would have liked that.

And what to do if something embarrassing happens. Like Diana told me about this author whose blouse came unbuttoned on national television and if it hadn't been for a quick-moving cameraman you would have seen right in her shirt. If that happened to me there would be nothing to see. But I still would DIE.

And what to do if the person interviewing you gets nasty and attacks you for something you wrote.

And what to do if someone in the audience asks a weird question, like what kind of underwear you're wearing.

Oh, the joy of thinking of all the humiliation that might lie ahead. . . . But then the fun really started.

14

If you could spend a day doing one of these things, which would you choose:

A. Getting a makeup lesson from the person who does the faces of Jennifer Love Hewitt and Jennifer Lopez and Jennifer Aniston? (*But not Sawyer's two Jennifers! Ha-ha!*)

B. Getting your hair cut and highlighted by the stylist who styles Julia Stiles?

C. Getting a whole new wardrobe on a shopping spree in New York City?

D. All of the above. (*Like ME ME ME!!!*)

That's right! It all happened to *me*! Can you say HEAVEN?!

I don't usually wear makeup (Mom's Rule Number 4,564). But in front of the camera you have to so you won't look all washed out or shiny. The makeup artist did my face for me three different ways to practice my interviews. I still looked pretty wholesome—Mom made sure of that.

But she let me get highlights! GO, MOM! Not anything crazy. But after getting my hair cut in a sharp shoulder-length bob, I got a few highlights. I was still dirty blond. Just a little less dirty.

And the shopping. Diana was the pro on this one.

"Let's hit Madison Avenue!" she said. "Today, we can go crazy!"

Wow. A dream come true. I was standing in front of Barneys, waiting to go in. I had been dreaming of this moment ever since I picked up my first fashion magazine. Every time I looked at one of those mags I thought, *if only* . . . And now it was coming true!

Except for one thing. I couldn't stop thinking of Sawyer showing off her $300 shoes all the time, and then making fun of everyone else's. And Myrna in her high-fashion ultra designer wear, being like, *Ha-ha I am so superior.*

Madison Avenue felt all wrong now. I mean, I was buying clothes to promote IS. And Isabella wouldn't think you had to spend a fortune to look good. (Isabella also wore Do It Yourself, but I would leave *that* for Harmony. I can only imagine what *I* would end up making. Yuk.)

After some discussion with Diana, I bought one sweater at Barneys that I totally loved. But just one. And then we jumped in a taxi and headed to SoHo to meet her niece, Zo. Zo goes to this fashion design college. Zo took us to all these out-of-the-way places where you could buy cool clothes that didn't cost as much. Then we went out to the suburbs and she showed me how to find the best things at the regular malls, the strip malls, the secondhand stores! It was a Totally Isabella Day.

"She has a good head on her shoulders, this one," Diana said, patting me on my shoulder. "She sticks to her values." My mom practically glowed.

I slept the whole train ride home. I was exhausted from shopping. When I checked my buddy list, I saw that Harmony was online, too.

Justme526: Shopping spree!!!

WhyteBubble: What did u get?

Justme526: 3 sweaters, 2 skirts, 2 pants, 1 cool jeans, 3 shoes. 2 earrings. 1 choker. 1 Gwyneth sighting. And 1 glam o rama dress for big nights out!

WhyteBubble: What big nights out? lol

Justme526: A girl can dream.

WhyteBubble: !!! Talked to dad. Kameelah's having trouble with reading in school. She's falling behind.

Justme526: ☹

WhyteBubble: Yeah . . . i wish i was there to help her. Hang on . . . Getting an IM . . . Oh it's Gabriela.

Justme526: ??

WhyteBubble: Leslie's kid. We're going 2 the movies soon.

Justme526: Kewl. Have fun. cya.

WhyteBubble: ttfn.

Mom came in and sat on my bed as I was signing off.

"I was very proud of you today. I was worried that this book business would get out of control. But Diana was right, you do have a good head on your shoulders," she said as she stroked my hair. I felt like I was six. But sometimes that's not a bad thing.

Magazine covers!

WHO IS IS?
And Why Does Every Girl
LOVE Her?!!

Fan mail!

Dear Jamie,
Your book CHANGED MY LIFE!
I LUV IT!!! ❤❤

Book reviews!

★★★★ Girls Will Stand Up
and Cheer for IS!
A MUST-READ!

~

This is where you probably came in. Because this is when it all went totally crazy. Did you first hear about me on the front page of *USA Today*? Maybe your mom saw the review in all the newspapers and got you the book? And then you started seeing it in *Seventeen*, *YM*, *Girls' Life*, *New Moon*, *CosmoGIRL!* . . . And then you saw Mary-Kate and Ashley tell Barbara Walters they had read a preview copy and it was the coolest thing they had ever read (besides their own books, of course). And then you saw the president's daughter wearing an *IS* T-shirt while she was riding the elephant in Africa.

But the weirdest thing, the craziest thing was . . .

OK, when I created IS, I felt powerful. I haven't ever felt like that in my entire life. IS totally rocked. But what was crazy was it was becoming more. I mean, I was starting to get emails:

```
Peaches12: Dear IS: These girls were
saying the shirt with the cat on it I
was wearing was so 3rd grade. And I
said I liked it and they go, Oooh she
thinks she's all that! But I just
Flicked them. And I was like yeah! I
like my cat shirt! So go away! And they
did.

MeggieH135: Hi IS! guess I should say
Jameson! I'm friends with this girl
```

```
who's always mean 2 me. After I read IS
I said to her, stop it already. And I
went Im going to Flick u if u don't.
And I told her to read ur book! So she
will know what Flick means!!!
```

I mean, the Flick was working. Really working. These girls were thinking IS was as awesome as I did! They felt that power that IS made me feel! They were saying something *I* wrote was changing their lives!

I didn't have time to make sense of it all. Oliver told me he was booking me for massive interviews. Until Mom told him to hold off for a week until midterms were over.

"So what are we supposed to tell *Teen People*? 'Sorry, she has to pass midterms before she can talk to you'?" I whined.

"Yes," said Mom. "That's exactly right."

"Sorry, kiddo," Dad said.

Ugh. My next book would include villains named Robin and Steven. Which, coincidentally, are my parents' names.

16

Customer Reviews

Write an online review and share your thoughts.

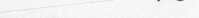

***** **You HAVE to read this book!**
Reviewer: BOOKGRL from Flagstaff, Arizona
IS is sooooooooo cooooooooool!!!!!!!!

"So," Connor asked me in study hall, "how's life as an author?"

"It's pretty good," I told him. "Aside from the fact that my parents won't let me do any interviews. Or let me spend any of the money from my book deal."

"Yeah," Connor said. "My parents won't let me either. Since I haven't been asked to do any interviews or made any money from my own book sales."

I smiled. Connor was pretty funny.

"I thought your book was great, by the way," Connor said.

"You read my book?" I asked, surprised.

"Well, yeah," Connor said. "It's not like every day somebody I know writes one. It really made me stop and think about all the things girls go through."

Well! That was nice! I felt myself turning red. OK, maybe we could talk about something else besides my book now.

"So, um," I said. "How about those Yankees?"

Then I saw Lindsay's face in the little window by the door. She was mouthing, "Jamie!" and waving her arms around.

I went up to the teacher's desk. Mr. "Scrambled" Eggleston looked at me.

"I really, really have to go." I crossed my legs for extra drama. I squirmed. He gave me the pass to the girls' room, and I went out to the hallway.

"I have gossip!" Lindsay dragged me down the hallway to a more private corner. "Big, major scoopage! Marco Vega and Sawyer Sullivan broke up! I heard Jennifer1 telling Jennifer2 about it. Sawyer told Marco they were over! O-V-E-R! She said she was never going to speak to him again!"

YES!!!

OK, not that that would really mean a whole lot for me. He was so way out of my league. But at least I wouldn't have to witness anymore Sawyer and Marco PDA!

Lindsay and I high-fived, and I went back into study hall. I sat at my desk. Sawyer had broken up with Marco. I wondered why. They were queen and king of our grade. Maybe she was going to go for a sophomore or junior or something? Anyway, this was huge news! The whole school was going to be buzzing about it soon.

The lunchroom did seem a little noisier than usual when suddenly, the intercom crackled over the whole entire school.

"Students, please listen up for a very important announcement," Principal Litagaki said.

Wow! The principal was going to announce that Sawyer and Marco had broken up. Even the principal thought it was big news. I mean, the last time he made an announcement was the bomb threat.

People started packing their backpacks to evacuate.

"We have just had word that one of our students has accomplished an incredible feat," Litagaki continued. "We are sure you are aware that our very own Jamie Bartlett has published a book. I am pleased to tell you that *IS* has just hit number one on the *New York Times* bestseller list. We at Whittaker High would like to extend our congratulations . . ."

NUMBER ONE? OK, number ONE??!!

I just sat there with my mouth hanging open. Not a pretty image, I know, but what would you do if your principal announced that your book hit number freakin' one on the *New York Times* bestseller list?

All of a sudden everyone started whistling and cheering and stuff. Lindsay was hugging me and screaming. Malik was, like, YEAH! Connor was cheering! My hand was red from all the high-fives. I'm number one! I'm number one!

Everything went wacko. The school let in all of these reporters to interview my friends and me. Lindsay told me Mr. Litagaki drove home and put on a suit really quick. He talked to as many reporters as he could. TV, newspapers, the works. I was so glad Diana had prepared me. I didn't even have time to get really nervous. Although I wished I had worn one of my new SoHo outfits instead of a regular T-shirt and jeans. At least the shirt was ice blue, one of the colors Diana had told me was on my personal color palette (with hot pink, coral, burgundy, and black). Red was so not on my color palette. I had come a looong way since my first newspaper interview outfit.

While Mr. Litagaki was practically giving a speech about how he was responsible for my success, I sneaked into the faculty ladies' room. I turned on my cell phone. Ten messages. Oliver, Mom, Harmony, Denise, Dad, Mom, Oliver, Harmony, Oliver, and Leslie.

"Jamie, call me, this is fantastic," Leslie said.

Denise said pretty much the same thing. "Early reports of your books sales are, well, I've never personally witnessed anything like this, Jamie."

Mom: "Sweetie! Do you need me there? I can be at your school in twenty minutes!"

Dad: "You were mentioned in the *Harvard Lampoon*! Did you hear that? Harvard!"

Harmony: "[Huge excited screaming sound!]"

Oliver: "I can have you booked up for the next millennium, babe. Your mom and Diana have the schedule, and they will go over it with you after school."

When the reporters finally left, it was time for English. Gallagher came over and hugged me. In front of everyone! I went redder than a human should be allowed to turn.

"Um, Miss Gallagher?" I said. "Thanks for everything."

I sat down at my desk trying to do what Diana told me. I smiled at each person's face to make them feel acknowledged. I nodded a little. I looked humble but appreciative. I kept my cool. Gallagher finally started class.

"Pssst!" Rebecca Ferman tossed me a note.

Jamie. Congrats. Very cool!!! Connor

I smiled.

"Jamie Bartlett?" some kid stuck his head in the doorway. "Principal Litagaki needs you."

This was becoming a habit. I jumped up. And tripped over my backpack. Everyone cracked up. I bolted.

My mom was in Principal Litagaki's office. She was all hyper as she told me that Oliver had called about something very, very big. I would be doing my first television interview, and it was scheduled for TOMORROW! No time to waste, I had to pack my bags. We were flying to Chicago. Because tomorrow, I was going to be on *Mora Live!*

~

IS admired the new ring sparkling on her finger. A good find at the flea market. Yes, it was the perfect fashion accessory for Flicking away Evil.

Her ring wasn't the only thing that was new. She'd been noticing something lately. Each time she Flicked, she was becoming more and more powerful.

Channel 6, 4:00 p.m.: Mora Live!
Fourteen-year-old bestselling author Jameson Bartlett talks frankly with Mora about being a young author and how her character IS is sweeping the nation and empowering girls.

So that was the long story to tell you how I got to be freaking out on *Mora Live!* And I survived. I smiled and did everything Diana had taught me. So now I know why she gets paid the big bucks. Because she can stop people from making fools of themselves on national TV. Dad watched it at home, and he said I did a good job. So did Oliver. It was all a huge relief.

By the time I got back home, I'd missed a day and a half of school. Mom dropped me off during my lunch period.

I caught up with Lindsay at the lunch line.

"Well? Did you see it?" I demanded.

"You were really good," Lindsay told me. "My mom taped the show, and we watched it when I got home."

"Thanks," I told her.

"What was it like? Were you freaking out?"

"Freaking out? Of course I was freaking out. Did you see the part where I knocked my microphone and it made that weird noise?" I moaned. "I mean, how typical ME. . . ."

"Yeah," Lindsay agreed. "That was a trauma-rama. But not as bad as the whole Sawyer thing."

The Sawyer thing?

What Sawyer thing?!

"Um, what Sawyer thing?" I asked slowly.

"You know, the part where you were talking about IS fighting the Evil One, and then you called Myrna 'Sawyer' by accident?" Lindsay said.

"I-I-I did what?! I called Myrna 'Sawyer' on NATIONAL TELEVISION?!" I could barely get the words out. I jumped up. "I am dead. I am so dead. I cannot be sitting here in this cafeteria. I have to get out of here!!"

"Is that JAMIE BARTLETT?" an unmistakable voice announced really, really loudly.

Lindsay gasped. It was too late. Sawyer had spotted me.

I. Was. So. Screwed. Lindsay shut her eyes. The sight of blood made her queasy.

Sawyer slithered on the bench right next to me. She put her arm around me. The Jennifers and the rest of the group were all watching.

"Um, hi, Sawyer," I squeaked.

"Jennifer was home sick yesterday with the flu," Sawyer said. "Isn't that sad?"

"Oh. Really sad." I nodded, stalling. "So, very, very sad."

"So she saw you on *Mora Live!*" Sawyer said. "And she taped it for me. I'm going to watch it tonight. Isn't that exciting? I'll let you know tomorrow what I think."

Lindsay sucked in her breath. I did, too.

And then Sawyer went back to her own table. I finally exhaled.

I. Am. So. Dead.

"Maybe she meant that in a nice way," Lindsay suggested doubtfully. "Maybe Jennifer also had an ear infection and her hearing was blocked. So Sawyer doesn't even know you called her evil on national television and she was just being, uh, excited for you."

"Oh come on, Linds," I said. "Sawyer Sullivan knows everything."

~

"National television star, eh?" Connor said, as we walked into English class. I was being extra careful not to go anywhere by myself. Maybe Sawyer hadn't seen it for herself, but if she knew what I'd said on TV . . . I just couldn't let down my guard. I needed witnesses in case I was attacked. I figured Sawyer wouldn't do it herself—she might break a nail. She would delegate the dirty deed. So I kept an extra eye out for a Jennifer. Lindsay had helped me check my locker for exploding devices. I also had Lindsay check my back between every class to make sure I didn't have a BEAT THE CRAP OUT OF ME sign on my back like Timothy Prichard did that one time at the pep rally.

"A lot of it is really fun," I said, answering Connor's question. "But a lot of it just makes me feel really nervous and stressed-out. I mean, I want people to read my book. But the whole media thing . . ."

Yeah. I was definitely not used to that. Cameras in my face. I felt like people were just waiting to see if I would say something dumb, do something dumb. Like, oh, say, call the most popular girl in the freshman class Evil.

"It's hard," I confessed.

"I could see that." Connor was thoughtful. "Especially since it all happened so fast. I mean one minute you're regular you. The next minute you're a famous author. That must be some pressure."

"Yeah!" I said. "People are treating me like I'm somebody different and like I'm supposed to know what I'm doing. It's really—"

"Connor! Connor! I need to talk to you!" Jennifer2 was coming down the hall.

"Oh, hey. Gotta go," Connor said.

"Yeah, OK," I said. I watched him walk over to Jennifer2. She was all happy to see him. He gave her a hug. Guess he was happy to see her, too.

I walked into English.

"Hiiiii, Jamie!" Sawyer waggled her manicured fingers at

me from her row in the S's. "Hope we don't have a lot of homework so I'll have time to watch your tape tonight!"

Oh nightmare. I slid into my seat and stared straight ahead as Miss Gallagher congratulated me on my *Mora Live!* performance. I tried to blank out everything going on with Sawyer. I needed a little pick-me-up. Something to brighten my mood. Marco Vega's legs. I would look at Marco Vega's legs.

Ahh, they looked so nice in those camouflage pants.

I watched as Marco Vega wrote a note. He folded it up and reached down and slid it to Tirrell Nelson. I waited for it to be slid over to Sawyer Sullivan.

But Trevor slid it to Priya Mahraza. Who shot it to Rebecca Ferman. Who tossed it on to my desk.

MY desk.

I waited until Gallagher was facing the L's and M's. I unfolded the note.

What's up. From Marco

It said WHAT'S UP!! I quickly double-checked the outside of the note. Yup, it said Jamie on it. Well, actually it said "Jamey." Close enough. It said WHAT'S UP!!

What's up! Marco Vega was asking me what was up!

I automatically turned around to catch Harmony's attention. But wait, it was her city month and her desk was empty. Where was Harmony when I needed her! Instead all I saw was one of the Jennifers giving me a suspicious look. Oops, she must have seen the Marco note thing. I snuck a look at Sawyer Sullivan. Sawyer was staring the other way, out the window. Whew. She would never know Marco had acknowledged my existence. That's all I needed. Sawyer Sullivan thinking I was trying to grab her ex on the rebound, on top of everything else.

The bell rang. I reached down to get my backpack off the floor when a pair of sneakers appeared in my face. I looked up to see really muscular legs. In camouflage pants.

"Dude."

Marco Vega.

18

"And then he walked out with me to my locker!" I told Harmony on the phone that night.

"What's the deal with him and Sawyer?" Harmony asked. So I filled her in about the breakup and the part about how Sawyer was going to kill me tomorrow after watching the *Mora Live!* tape.

"But no, she didn't see Marco walk me to my locker," I said. "Whew."

"Jamie, be careful," Harmony warned.

Well, OK. OBVIOUSLY this was the deal.

Marco was only paying attention to me because I was getting famous. Like in that book where the girl finds out she's a princess and the guy goes out with her because he wants to be famous? Like I was supposed to be so blinded by Marco's gorgeous face and bod that I thought he was in love with my inner beauty or something.

Duh. I may not have a chest, but I do have a brain.

But . . . OK . . .

Wasn't there a chance, a small chance, that it really was

the whole "Marco is a poet and now he has recognized me as his literary soul mate, and realizes I am his destiny" thing?

"Just watch your back," Harmony warned me. "I have to go. I'm meeting Gabriela at Starbucks. IM you later."

"Bye."

Oh yeah. That reminded me. I needed to fix my email so I could IM with Harmony. For some reason, my email password wasn't working and I couldn't sign on. I hate that. I called tech support. Thanks to the corded phone, I was attached to the wall on hold for an hour.

They told me I had changed my password.

"I didn't change my password," I said. My password should still be MVIASLB. (Marco Vega Is A Sexy Love Beast.)

Well. I didn't tell them that last part.

The tech girl told me that my password had definitely been changed from my own home computer. It was now BiteMe. Weird! It took us twenty minutes to get my account sorted out. What a mess.

How could my password have been changed from my own computer? I mean no one uses the computer except Allie. But she has her own screen name and wouldn't know my password. Plus she's too dumb anyway. Duh-mb. Duh-g. Maybe it was Duh. That was it. Allie's boyfriend was over last night. He must have some hacker quality I didn't catch.

Allie must have somehow gotten Duh to change my password. I was really ticked. I mean, a password is a sacred thing.

I was already pissed off at Allie for what she'd said at dinner the other night. My dad goes, "So did you write anything today, Jamie? I'm sure colleges would be impressed if you were more than a one-hit wonder."

And Allie goes, "Yeah, she wrote a love note to Marco Vega." Then she made kissy noises.

So of course Dad and Mom are like, "Who's Marco Vega?"

And I'm all, "Oh no one," while kicking Allie under the table.

Allie said, "Marco Vega is the most popular freshman guy, right, Jamie?"

"Oh!" Mom got kind of happy that I might possibly have a remote chance of getting a boyfriend someday. She is so totally out of it sometimes. "Is he the quarterback of the football team?"

"No, Mom, and that is so nineteen-fifties," I told her. "The most popular guy does *not* have to be a football player. He's even way cooler than a football player. And I'm sure he's smarter since he isn't getting his head knocked around." (I said that last part for Allie's benefit. I had nothing against the sport but her BF Duh was on the football team. She glared at me.)

"Oh, I see," said Dad. "He's like Fonzie. You know, from *Happy Days?* The boy in the leather jacket who was too cool for school? With the motorcycle? And the bad attitude?"

"Yeah, Dad," Allie, Nick at Nite rerun queen, egged him on. "Marco Vega is just like the Fonz." She stuck her thumb up and went, "Ayyyy."

"Well, then, Jamie. I don't think you should be dating a boy like that," said Mom sternly. "This Marco Vega sounds like bad news."

"Mooom," I wailed. "I am so NOT dating Marco Vega. Not that I wouldn't want to go out with him—if he would ask me! But he would never go out with *me!*"

"Damn straight," Allie muttered under her breath.

"Well," said Dad, "then the issue is closed. No Marco Vega for you."

Well, back then I thought my dad's ban on Marco Vega didn't make a difference anyway. It all seemed so impossible. But that was before the whole note passing/Marco Vega walking me to my locker thing.

So thanks to Allie, I had just spent a whole evening glued to the kitchen phone waiting for tech support to fix my email AND my parents thought Marco Vega was a rebel outlaw.

AND Sawyer Sullivan was probably right now watching the *Mora Live!* tape. Plotting how to kill me. Or, worse, how to humiliate me at school tomorrow.

~

The Ostracizor sneered. "Sorry, this lunch table is saved. Dorks sit over at that table." But then she turned around and gasped. IS had appeared!

Before she could say anything, the Ostracizor was flung—splat!—right into a vat of meat loaf surprise.

Channel 4 News at Noon!
Thanks for the weather, Bo. And coming up at the bottom of the hour, an interview with someone who knows the inside details on how a local bestselling author got her inspiration!

~

Lindsay and I walked into the cafeteria.

"You look left, I'll look right," I said nervously.

"I don't see her," Lindsay said. "I swear."

I had been lucky so far. No sign of Sawyer Sullivan. Maybe she'd stayed home from school, and I could live one more day. I'd tried to fake being sick myself. But Dad reminded me I'd missed school for *Mora Live!* and that newspaper interview, and the other interview and *blah blah*, even if I had pneumonia I better get to school immediately or I would never get into a decent college.

We moved through the hot-lunch line.

"Turkey burger and fries," I told the lunch lady.

"Get the cheese fries. They rock."

I jumped. The voice in my ear was . . . Marco Vega's.

"Um, OK, cheese fries," I squeaked. My heart was pounding. I moved through the line, and Marco moved with me. Lindsay looked at me like, *Huh?!!*

"Hey, Jamie," Marco said. "You guys come on over to our table. You can share your cheese fries with me."

And he walked away.

Did he say what I thought he said?

"Oh my gosh," Lindsay said. "Did Marco Vega just invite you to eat lunch with him?"

"He did! He did!" I said. "OK, what do I do? What do I do?"

"I don't know," Lindsay said, paying for her lunch. "This could be the sneak attack you've been waiting for. Sawyer might have put him up to it."

I looked over at the Freshman Popular Table. I saw the Jennifers, a couple of football players . . . no Sawyer.

"I think she's absent today," I said. "Plus, they broke up, remember? What do you think I should do?"

"I don't know about this," Lindsay said doubtfully. "Going over there is pretty risky. Could be a trap. Could be a joke."

OK, OK, OK, she's right. I'm not thinking clearly. Being that close to Marco is fuzzing up my brain. I should just go over to our regular table. Me and Ol' Linds. Just like usual.

But Marco had invited me to sit with him! How could I resist?!! He's just so freakin' HOT. I have to go over! There's a magnetic pull or something.

"Jamie! Where are you going!"

Lindsay was not feeling the pull. Think fast, Jamie.

"OK, OK," I said. "How 'bout this. We casually walk past their table and see what happens. If Marco just happens to notice us and call us over, we'll go."

"Not we. You," Lindsay said. "That's all the Popular People. I can't crash that. I'd be laughed out of Whittaker."

"But Marco invited you, too," I whined.

"Jamie, noooooo," she said.

"Please?" I begged. Lunch period was passing by! I was going to miss my chance!

"Please, please, oh pleasy please, Lindsay, my wonderful friend, oh please please please. . . ." I was not too proud to beg.

I had to take action. I started walking toward their table . . . and Lindsay followed me.

That's the great thing about Lindsay—she is always there when you need her. And she cracks easily, too.

So la, li, la, we walked past our usual table and close to the Popular Table. Closer, closer, OK, Marco notice me . . .

"Hey, Jamie! Over here!" Marco said. YEEEEessss!!!!! Victory! He slid over, making room for me! (And Lindsay. Who looked terrified as we sat down.)

"Um, hi?" I said to everyone. I got a couple hi's back. Jennifer1 didn't look at me. Jennifer2 looked confused. Everyone else was like *hey*, or ignored us and kept on talking.

"I feel really stupid," Lindsay whispered to me.

"Can I have some of your cheese fries?" Marco asked me. Of course! Yes! Anything! He moved closer to grab some fries.

And I felt his leg bump into mine. Things got a little blurry. Marco pressing up against me made me light-headed.

Marco was talking to a basketball player about cars. They were all *Porsche Mercedes Lamborghini*. And Marco said to me, "Which one do you like best?"

And I got to talk to him! I said, "Um, Maserati?" Marco said, "Cool." I guess I hadn't given a stupid answer!

But that was all I said. Because I was way too nervous. Plus they were all talking about some sophomore party they all went to. I did notice Allie, sitting with Duh at her table, look over. She was, like, *what??* Jamie at the Popular Table?

And I got to watch Marco out of the corner of my eye. I wished we could eat lunch together alone. He could recite poetry to me, while I fed him cheese fries. He would see that I was the only girl who could truly appreciate his inner poet, not just his outer studmuffin-ness.

"Nobody's talking to me," Lindsay whispered. "Can we leave now?"

"Not yet!" I hissed. Lindsay must be sacrificed. Sitting next to Marco all nice and cozy. I would make it up to Lindsay later. I wanted it to last and last. Then the bell rang. Way too soon.

"See ya in English," Marco said to me.

"Lindsay," I said, as we walked out of the cafeteria. "Marco Vega's leg was next to mine!"

"I'm so happy for you," Lindsay said. "But I hope we don't have to do it again tomorrow. It's difficult to enjoy my lunch with cheerleaders whispering and laughing at my sweatpants."

"Oh, I'm sorry. That sucked for you. I owe you big," I said. Lindsay went to her class, and I walked through the halls alone. I was letting down my guard a little, since it looked like Sawyer was absent today.

What a great day. Marco Vega! The Popular Table! (Well, OK. Eating at the popular table wasn't all it was cracked up to be. It *was* kinda fun to see Allie's face when she saw me there. And I didn't humiliate myself or anything. But other than that, nothing Earth-shattering.)

I was still all happy when I got to history class. The lights were off, which was great since I was late and could sneak into my seat. The TV monitor was on. A historical video? Perfect. I needed a nap after staying up all night worrying about Sawyer Sullivan attacks. I put my head down.

"Welcome to *News at Noon* with Gail," the television was saying. "And welcome to our special guest today, Sawyer Sullivan. Sawyer is not only a close and personal friend of bestselling author Jameson Bartlett, but she's the inspiration behind her book. Nice to have you here, Sawyer."

Excuse me? Was I dreaming? Did I fall asleep already? I lifted my head up off my desk.

"Nice to be here, Gail," Sawyer was saying. Well, that explains why she wasn't in school today trying to kill me.

"So tell us how you inspired a major character in a bestselling book?" this Gail person asked.

What the??? Yes, Sawyer, tell us. How did you inspire?

"Well, Jameson based one of the characters on me," Sawyer said. "It was a complete surprise."

"How exciting. And flattering—I see in my notes the character is described as having 'gorgeous shiny hair and a perfect body.'"

"Well." Sawyer looked all modest. "It's true. The rest of the character of course was made up to give the story some conflict."

It only got worse. Sawyer talked about how she was in my English class. And how I'd always admired her. And how flattered she was to be such an inspiration to me. Augh!

"Congratulations, Sawyer. It's been a pleasure talking with you today."

"Thank you, Gail."

I heard applause from the front of the room.

"How fabulous did Sawyer look?" Jennifer1 squealed. "That tweed suit was to *die* for!"

I flopped my head back down on the desk. Ugh. How does she do it? How is it possible that I based an *evil villain* on this girl, and she still managed to make herself look like that's a good thing? And she looked great on TV, too. She didn't even need a media coach, two hairdressers, or a makeup artist. Figures.

Bzzzt. My pager went off. I read the text message.

Jamie. Last-minute change of plans. Your mother will be there to pick you up at the front of the school in 10 minutes. You're going to be flying out tonight to attend the Teen Yes Awards in California. Oliver.

20

TO JAMESON BARTLETT AND PARENT OR GUARDIAN

ADMIT ONE PLUS GUEST

teen yes awards

LOS ANGELES, CALIFORNIA

~

My mom was waiting for me at the front of the school. She didn't say a word, just handed me the invitation.

OMG. The Teen Yes Awards. You know, the hottest celebrities, the red carpet, the paparazzi.

One minute, I'm sitting in history class flipping out over Sawyer's interview. The next minute, I'm sitting in *first* class on my way to L.A. Can you believe it? Yes, I was a last-minute invite on the studio's part, but who cares! I mean, I wasn't going to get an award or anything. But I'm one of the "invited guests," the guy told my mom, meaning they want to fill as many seats with teen-oriented celebrities as possible. Wow! I'm considered a "teen-oriented celebrity"!!!

Oh. And I wasn't selling out, you know, going Hollywood. OK, maybe the awards were a bit frivolous. Hottest Male Celebrity, Best Onscreen Smooch. But hey, when you get a good grade on a test you're supposed to reward yourself, like with a sundae or a long nap or something. When your journal accidentally becomes a bestselling novel, shouldn't you be able to reward yourself with an all-expenses-paid trip to a star-studded Hollywood extravaganza without guilt?

And it was good to escape Sawyer's wrath for a little longer. Very good. Even though she claims to the local viewing audience we're close personal friends, I'm pretty sure she'll still attempt to get me.

But on the other hand I *didn't* want to leave because . . .

Marco Vega Interactions! Marco walked with me in the hall for a little ways. For real! I was so excited I told him I was going to the Teen Yes Awards and he goes, "L.A.! That's a cool place to go!" He said he wanted to live there and be like Ben Affleck someday. But Connor was also walking with us and he goes, "You want to be an actor, Marco? You should try out for the class play." And Marco got all horrified, like, "With the drama geeks?" and walked quickly ahead of us.

But then Marco turned around and said, "Say hi to the movie stars!" And we were waving at each other, like, Goodbye! Good-bye! And I thought for one second, how can I go all the way across country and leave MARCO VEGA as a single man!

But I will be back, Marco. Wait for me.

All right, I had to stop thinking about Marco. Even I could tell when I was too obsessed.

I leaned back in my cushy seat with extra legroom. I thought about what a crazy week it had been. My book had popped up on all these bestseller lists. I talked on some radio shows about IS. I talked to lots of reporters from magazines and newspapers.

We were at cruising altitude, and all portable electronic devices could be used. So I took out my new laptop and started it up.

Oh yeah! I forgot to say this! I GOT A NEW LAPTOP! So I could keep up with my homework and stuff while I was traveling. Oh, don't go thinking I got the Maserati Spyder or anything. Just the laptop. Still, for my family, that was HUGE.

I checked my personal email. There was one from Malik.

```
To:     JustMe526
From:   ThaMan3995


James! RU reading this in Cali?!! Me
Connor & Linds took bets out on u:
Odds of u seeing NSYNC: 2 to 1
Odds of u within 5 feet of Brad and
Jennifer: 4 to 1
Odds of u talking 2 Josh Hartnett: 15
to 1 (although Linds gave me 13 to 1
since she knows you'll b stalking him)
```

```
Odds of Josh Hartnett talking back 2 u:
22 to 1 since he would know u were
stalking him
Odds of u tripping on the red carpet: I
say YES U WILL! (Connor says NO. Linds
passed.)


Ha-Ha! 20 bucks if u say MALIK'S THE
MAN on TV!


Malik.
```

Now there's a vote of confidence.

Next, I checked my new screen name for my "business," IsFlix. I needed a "business" email because I was getting more fan mail! From real live fans!

```
KCSparkles: Hey! I luv yr book! IS is 2
kewl! Flick! Flick! Write me back! :)-
TTFN!


FLICKgrrrl: Dear Jameson, how did you
come up with Isabella? How do you think
of your ideas? Do you think you will
write another Isabella book?


Altan8: Hi. IS was really great. My
life sucks right now. My best friends
```

```
are leaving me out of everything. I
didn't make cheerleading. My parents are
fighting. I gained 3 pounds. Everything
sucks!
```

Ouch. That last one was pretty sad. What could I say to her to make her feel better? I really do want to help her . . . um, um. . . . I chewed on my fingernail. Oops, I could hear Diana's voice in my head, *No Chewing, Jamie.* Besides, I want my nails to look good for the Teen Yes Awards! I'd be getting a manicure tomorrow and everything! I was thinking a pale pink would look nice with my dress. Maybe with a little sparkle. Are sparkly nails in? Maybe they're out this year. I should stick with the plain, not sparkly, to be on the safe side.

OK, wait, train of thought here. In like two seconds I went from trying to empower poor Altan8 to obsessing about my nails.

I went back to answering Altan8 and told her to hang in there. Talk to someone about her feelings. Maybe try to make a new friend. I emailed her that Isabella would send her some Flicks. Not the greatest advice. But not the worst. Please let the next email be easier.

```
QuinnieD: Dear IS! Ur book is the
BEST!!!!!! Wuv, Q
```

Oh yeah. Much better. Really, this was very fairy tale. My agent, my editor, my publicist, and my mom had all drilled me on how hard it was to get a book published—even for *real* writers. I was like a freak of nature, the one-in-a-million combo of good timing and having a teacher with connections.

When I stood up to go to the *first-class* bathroom, I noticed a girl a few rows back. She was reading *IS*, and she was smiling.

At that moment I really, really loved my book.

Channel 11, 9:00 p.m.: The third annual
Teen Yes Awards will be aired live
from Hollywood, California.

~

The morning of the Teen Yes Awards was a major blur. The salon at the hotel did my hair, nails, and makeup. My dress was pressed. (Thank you, Diana, for talking me into buying the lavender flippy dress with a little bit of sparkly in it.) I have dangly earrings and silvery shoes. I think I look very Mandy Moore.

I was ready. I just had to walk down a carpet and smile.

IN FRONT OF ALL OF THESE CAMERAS! AND STARS! AND ON NATIONAL TELEVISION! I was freaking myself out. Mom saw my look.

"You'll be fine, honey. We're here to have fun," she said. "Maybe you'll get lucky and a Backstreet Boy will sneeze on you."

Har, har, har, Mom.

~

When we got to the amphitheater, the limo driver helped me out.

There it was—the red carpet. The flashbulbs were popping. I heard people calling, "Beyoncé!" "Hillary!" "Ashton!" "Raven!" "Kirsten!"

I walked the way Diana taught me. Head up, smile on. No one was yelling *Jamie! Jamie!* That was a *good* thing at this point. I was having enough trouble walking just being anonymous. Especially since I was now walking BEHIND AMBER TIFFANY! Yes, it was the real Amber Tiffany! (Or the sort-of-real Amber Tiffany. You know, those implants and all.)

"Amber! Amber!" the photographers were shouting. She stopped and gave a little pout, a little pose. She was wearing a denim dress cut down to *there* and black cowboy boots. And a little tiara in her hair.

"Isn't that the girl hanging up in your room?" my mom whispered.

Yes, Mom. And the girl who had sent me over the edge. The girl who, in a way, was responsible for Isabella. I checked her out. She was even skinnier in person.

"She needs to eat something," my mom said, disapproving. "And put on some clothes."

We were reaching the end of the red carpet. Suddenly Malik's message popped into my head.

No! I had made it! I stepped off the red carpet. I had made it without tripping!

My heel caught the very edge of the red carpet. *Bam!* Down I went.

~

"OMG OMG!" Lindsay was screaming. "I saw the show!!!"

I tried to call Harmony on my cell the minute the awards show was over, but she wasn't picking up. So I called Lindsay. The awards had been shown live and of course, I wanted to know one thing. . . .

"Was I on TV?"

"YES!" shrieked Lindsay.

"What was I doing?!?" I demanded, praying it wasn't the trip *off* the red carpet. Hm, if I tripped *off* the carpet did that mean Malik or Connor won the bet?

"You were in the audience and they close-upped on you," Lindsay told me. "It even said *Jameson Bartlett, Bestselling Author* under your face! Hey, your hair looked awesome! How come you don't do it like that for school?"

Er, because I don't have two hairstylists at my beck and call to do me up for a big day on the red carpet of Whittaker High School.

"Did you see Josh Hartnett? *Did you?!*" Lindsay could barely control herself, I could tell.

I reeled off all the stars I saw and listened to Lindsay scream. I told her about the photographers calling my name after the show. And the goodie bag everyone got filled with CDs, makeup, sunglasses.

"And I didn't even tell you the best part!!! Guess where

I'm going right this very minute?!" I had received an invitation to an After the Awards Party. And we were walking over there now! I did try to ditch Mom, but the invite said, "And Guest." Who was I kidding? Like Mom was going to let me go Hollywood without a chaperone anyway.

When we arrived at the place where the after-party was I said good-bye to Lindsay. (After she made me promise about twelve times to tell her every minute detail when I got home.)

"Name?" Huge Door Guy said.

"Jamie Bartlett. And mother," I added lamely. He looked down the list. He looked some more. I started to get nervous. What if I wasn't really invited?

"Jameson? You're in," he said. "Put this on."

He gave my mom a blue plastic bracelet and me a red one.

"Doesn't he know red clashes with lavender?" I asked Mom, once we were safely out of hearing range.

"I think red means you are underage. So you can't have alcohol," Mom told me.

"Oh." I'd be quiet now. So I didn't say anything stupid around all the celebrities.

We followed the crowd into the other room. A girl offered us drinks. I got a soda and sipped it. I felt kind of dumb standing there with my mother. I looked at all the celebrities standing around talking to each other. I didn't know one person. Except my mother.

"Jamie! I think that's George Jackson!" my mom gasped and pointed toward the pool. She pointed to an older guy who I recognized from one of the seventies CDs she played all the time.

"Go talk to him, Mom," I told her. Why not? It would give my mom the thrill of a lifetime.

"Oh, I can't," she gasped. But she Isabella'd. She went over and kind of stood near George Jackson. I could tell she was all ga-ga.

Well, that left me standing there by myself. Better or worse than standing with my mother? You tell me. I sipped my soda. La, la, la. I'm alone and mysterious, I told myself. Not a loser. There were these big couches. I decided to go sit on the one kind of close to a group of people and pretend like I belonged there. I was, um, waiting for my date or something. Yeah, that's it. The couch was comfy. I sank back on the cushion.

"Ow!" I said at the same time someone else did. My hair was caught! My hair was caught! On what? I tried to turn around and see. My hair was caught on . . . Amber Tiffany's tiara.

And she didn't look too happy about it.

22

"I'm really sorry—my hair must have gotten caught in your tiara," I babbled.

"Well, now my hair is all messed up," Amber Tiffany said. "Come to the ladies' and help me." She kind of demanded it and I did feel bad.

"Um, sure," I said. I guess I could help Amber Tiffany fix her tiara. Since I had ruined it and all.

We wove our way through the crowd and walked into the ladies' room. It was packed. I stood next to Amber Tiffany and waited while she fixed her hair in the mirror. I wasn't sure what I was supposed to be doing.

"Your tiara is nice," I said politely.

"Thank you," Amber Tiffany said as she moved her tiara back and forth. To the exact millidegree of perfection. Or maybe she just wanted extra time to look at her face in the mirror.

There was more silence, while she searched for something in her purse. Lipstick.

"I'm Jamie Bartlett," I said to her.

"Yes, hi," Amber Tiffany answered. Obviously she was not a big IS fan. I wondered if she could even read. "Could you hold my purse for a sec?" She didn't seem to feel the need to introduce herself back. I guess everyone knew who she was.

"Ugh," Amber Tiffany said, turning her back to the mirror. "My butt looks big."

What???!!!

"Yeah, right," I said to her. "You look great."

"I wish," she sighed.

"Jameson Bartlett!" someone said.

This girl on the other side of Amber Tiffany came over to me. "You *are* Jameson Bartlett, right?" She started Flicking at me.

Hey, it was Cadyn Christopher! You know, the one who plays nasty Brooke Brentley on *Brentley Street*. Harmony and I watch it every Tuesday night! We are practically members of the I Hate Brooke club. I backed away. The last time I saw Cadyn, she was putting poison in sweet Stephanie Chandler's pink lemonade.

"I recognize you from *Mora Live!* I *love* your book! I read it between shooting my scenes!" Cadyn said. "It's so awesome to meet you!"

"Hi, well, thanks," I said. Amber Tiffany looked at me with a little more interest. Maybe now she thought I was somebody.

"Can I have my bag back?" Amber Tiffany asked me. Or maybe she just wanted her bag back.

"I need to get this makeup off," Cadyn said, scrubbing at

her face. "It took like six layers to cover up my zits today."

I couldn't help but notice she was right. Without all her makeup, she looked pretty splotchy. I thought about what Harmony had said about all the lighting and makeup tricks that make everyone on TV look so good.

"So, Jameson!" Cadyn said happily. "Are you here with a ton of book people?" Cadyn asked. "Or do you want to come sit with us?!"

"Um, sure!" I said.

"Well, let's get out of here before we drown in cover-up." She waved to the girls at all the mirrors. There *were* a lot of concealer wands flying around.

I said bye to Amber Tiffany, but she was too busy adjusting her, um, front.

I looked for Mom on the way out. She was now *talking* to George Jackson. She was laughing. Hey. I think my mom was FLIRTING with him. Ew, I so did not want to see that.

Cadyn led me over to this big couch and introduced me to some people. There was Kimberlee Hays, who played Stephanie Chandler and didn't seem to be worried that Cadyn was going to poison her. And hey! Ryder Donovan, from *RoboMan III* and *Perfect Family*. He looked even hunkier in real life.

I sat down with them. Wow! I talked to Cadyn and Kimberlee for a little bit. Cadyn told Kimberlee about her favorite scenes. It was so cool.

"If they make a movie of it, tell them I'd be a great Isabella!" Cadyn said.

"I'll let them know!" I told her, laughing.

"I think it's really great how you're trying to help total losers and fat chicks feel better about themselves," Kimberlee said. "Give them their moment of glory flicking some evil diva!"

Well, I wouldn't have put it quite like that. . . .

Then Amber Tiffany came over and sat down next to me. She gave me a big air kiss like this: *Kiss! Kiss!* Near my cheek but not on me. Like we were best buds Hollywood style or something. Phooooony. Still, it was kind of exciting. Would anyone believe this? This was the time I wished for a photographer! Was I dying to get my picture taken with this group or what?! Even a nostril shot!

"So I hear you wrote a book," Amber Tiffany said. For a girl with such hot looks, she sure had a dud of a voice. She sounded like she wouldn't get excited over anything.

"Yeah," I said, feeling really shy. I mean, she was on my bedroom *wall*! But I wasn't going to tell her *that*.

Before I could say anything at all, she started talking. She talked about the outfit she was going to wear tonight but the designer wasn't appreciative enough so she changed. That'll show him. And she complained about having to sit next to some B-list actor at the awards show. And how come the waitress was taking so long to come back with her sparkling water, this was so typical.

I covered up a yawn. Amber Tiffany was really . . . boring. Whine, whine, *whine*.

"But isn't it cool to be here?" I asked her.

"I didn't even *win* anything," she whined.

Amber Tiffany is coming down off my wall. ASAP. I wouldn't be able to look at her again without getting a headache.

I looked around for Mom. She was still standing with George Jackson and his trio. They were holding out a microphone. Oh, great. Mom and karaoke? Let's hope not.

Then, Ryder came over. He sat in between Amber Tiffany and me.

"Hey, Babe," he said to Amber Tiffany. Then he turned to me. "Hello, Beautiful Stranger."

OMG! RoboMan called me Beautiful Stranger!

Lindsay and Harmony will die when I tell them this. I wished everyone from school could see me now sitting next to Ryder Donovan. Hm. I checked my watch for New York time. Three hours later. Late enough for Dad to be asleep. But early enough for Allie to think it was for her and grab the phone. Might as well take advantage of this.

I dialed home. Allie whispered hello, knowing she'd get in trouble for answering so late.

"Hey, Allie Pallie!" I said cheerfully. "It's me!"

"Oh, what do *you* want?" she snarked. "I saw you on TV. Did you know you had a big hunk of food in your teeth?" Nice try, Allie, but I knew I didn't. I'd checked. And had Mom recheck. "Back at the hotel early after too much excitement today for little loser Jamie?"

"Actually I'm at the after-party," I said. "Hang on a sec." I turned to Ryder.

"I don't mean to be obnoxious, but do you mind saying hi to my sister back in NY?" I asked him. He took the phone.

"Hey, what's up there, Sister?" Ryder said. He paused for a minute. "Ryder. Ryder Donovan. No, really. I was at Teen YES today. Um, blue shirt, black pants . . ."

I heard Allie scream. She loves Ryder Donovan. I mean luuuuuuuuuuuvs him. He's been Allie's favorite star even before RoboMan. Allie and I used to watch him together when he played Mikey, the brother on *Perfect Family*. When we would talk about our futures, she always wanted to marry Ryder. I would always call her "Mrs. Donovan." I mean, back when we were friends.

And look at me, all sitting next to him. I took the phone back.

"I'm back," I said.

"Was that for real?" Allie said. "Was that really Ryder Donovan?"

"Yup," I said all casually. "What, Ryder? Gotta go, Ryder's saying something to me." I hung up.

I'm hanging out with my sister's favorite star! In Hollywood! While she's sitting at home. Dad's probably having her fill out financial aid forms for college. Poor Allie.

Oh, what the heck.

"Um, I know this is cheesy but can I also get your autograph for my sister?" I asked Ryder. I got a pen out of my purse.

"Hey, no prob," he said.

"For Allie," I told him. "With an *i-e*." And I told him what else to write, too.

"Well, I hate to break up the party but I have an early call tomorrow," Cadyn said. "I can't catch a break even on Saturday." She gave me her email and I gave her mine. We promised to keep in touch. I couldn't believe I was hugging the Evil Brooke Brentley good night.

Let's review!

The Evil Brooke Brentley is really nice. Amber Tiffany is a total waste of oxygen. I can talk to Ryder Donovan without stuttering, throwing up, burping, or otherwise making a fool of myself.

I have successfully conquered Hollywood!

Pretty cool. I laid back on the couch and smiled.

"So what happens is that the social outcasts, you know—like, nerds and fat chicks and losers—do this flicking thing with their hands. And then the popular girls give up."

Kimberlee was sitting behind me, talking about my book—even though she wasn't getting it exactly right. Still sort of cool.

"So it's fiction, right?" some girl's voice I didn't recognize said.

"Duh, obviously. Like that ever happens in real life, the fat chicks and losers winning out. Maybe they walk away thinking they made a difference, but they never do."

Or maybe not so cool. What was Kimberlee saying? That wasn't the way it was in my book.

"I know." The other girl giggled. "Like this morning, this

huge girl came on to the set trying to be an extra. And Jean-Paul was like, um, honey, you don't have the right look for this scene. And the girl was like, you should have girls of all sizes in the background. And Jean-Paul was all, OK, sweetie. Whatever you say. She's all like, Ha! I win! And then Jean-Paul edited the film with her out of it!"

Kimberlee and the girl started cracking up.

Sweet Stephanie Chandler was starting to sound like Sawyer Sullivan.

"Well, the author's fourteen. What does she know? And she's not exactly a supermodel herself, so you know. It probably makes her feel good writing stuff like that," Kimberlee said. "These girls need to believe they have a chance."

I felt tears prick at my eyelids. OK, true, I'm not a supermodel. I don't look like Kimberlee or Amber Tiffany. I didn't need to hear that, though.

I should just ignore them. I know, I know. I shouldn't listen to them. But I couldn't help thinking of Sawyer always making fun of me, taking credit on TV, being popular even though she was a bitch. Maybe they were right. Maybe I was stupid, maybe IS was, too. Maybe these girls did always win in the end.

I suddenly felt really, really tired.

Ryder Donovan came over to me. He didn't notice that my eyes were all red.

"Hey, Author! Isn't that your manager dancing on the piano bar with those old guys over there?"

I looked where he was pointing. OMG. My mother was

doing "YMCA" with George Jackson and the George Jackson Trio. People were clapping and cheering and waving their arms around. "Y—M—C—A." Oh no. I couldn't look.

This night was turning out to be WAY humiliating. And about to get worse, I thought, as the first notes of the chicken dance started. I made my way through the crowd toward Mom.

It was time for this bestselling author to get her mother off the piano bar and go back home.

Q: If you had to be trapped
in an elevator with one of these animals,
which would you choose?

A. A lion
B. A bear
C. A shark
D. A gorilla

Malik picked B) bear. He claimed he could wrestle the bear down. Right. Malik is like 100 pounds—and 50 of them are his mouth.

Yes, I was back to reality. Sitting with Connor and Malik in study hall. It was Monday after the L.A. trip, and I was still feeling kind of buzzy from it. I lobbied Mom for a day off. No go. The mom singing on the piano bar was back to the mom who wouldn't let me miss piano lessons.

"Is there water in the elevator?" Connor asked. "Because if there wasn't, definitely a shark."

I took a second to picture being trapped in an elevator all right, but with Marco Vega. He would say, "It appears the elevator is not working." And he would sweep me into his arms and start kissing me. And then he would go all James Bond and break through the roof. And carry me to safety.

It was only first period, so I hadn't seen Marco Vega yet. But I was waiting.

"What about you, Jamie?" Malik asked me. "Lion, bear, shark, or gorilla?"

"Speaking of sharks, Jamie, tell us about L.A.," Connor said.

I gave Connor and Malik the basic rundown—the award show, the after-party. I skipped the Kimberlee part. And the Mom-on-the-piano-bar part.

"Man. You saw Amber Tiffany," Malik said. "Man oh man."

"Wow, that sounds like you were total Hollywood," Connor said.

"Well, just for the weekend," I said. That was all I could handle. I was still bumming about what Kimberlee had said.

The bell rang, and Lindsay met me out in the hall.

"I like your outfit," Lindsay said. "Is that new?"

"Yeah, I got it that one time in the city. But ugh, I practically had to squeeze on these jeans today," I told her. "I must have eaten too much in California. I was on an oinkfest."

"Oh," Lindsay said, looking uncomfortable. Then she brightened. "Anyway, can you believe like practically yesterday you were hanging out with movie stars? And now you're back here at boring old Whittaker?"

"I know. It's so weird. It's like, did all that really happen? It's like this weird dream."

"I'll never get to hang out with movie stars." Lindsay sighed. "I'm lucky you guys will even be my friends." Lindsay sighed a bigger sigh. "I mean, *you're* hanging out with movie stars in Hollywood. Harmony will probably *be* a star, she's already so glamorous. Or at least president. And then there's me. Just like on TV, there's always the fat friend hanging around in the background." Another sigh.

"Uh, what was that last part?" I asked her. OK, for a minute I thought I'd spotted Marco Vega down the hall.

"See? I'm such a loser even my friends won't listen to me."

"No," I told her. "I'm being a bad friend. You're having a bad day and I'm not helping. I'm sorry."

"I wish IS would just come along and you know, do her change-the-world thing. Make it so that looking like me and being me wasn't so pathetic," Lindsay said.

"You *don't* look pathetic. At least you have a chest!" OK, lousy attempt at humor.

But Lindsay wasn't laughing anything off. She started to spew. "My father was at it again last night. My mom was putting dessert on the table and he gave her that *look*, like don't give Lindsay any. So she put my cake in front of Jared, who was practically laughing out loud at me. Of course then I had to take a slice and inhale it just to tick my father off. And he told me I was pathetic and he was going to the gym and if I had any self-respect I would go, too."

"Lindsay, that's awful," I said. "You really should say something to your mom. Maybe she can help."

"My mom? She went off to the gym with him. That's when I heard him say I was a pig with no self-control. Then my mom goes, 'All girls get more padding around puberty and Lindsay is healthy and her doctor said there's nothing to worry about if she's exercising and eating right and whatever.' And my dad goes, 'Yeah, right. Oink oink.'"

Whoa. Poor Lindsay. That was some serious pressure. Her mom was so skinny and always running off to some class at the gym. I guess who wouldn't be, when you're worrying that the guy you married is so into looks.

"Lindsay, that's terrible," I said to her. I tried to think of something helpful to say. I wished, for the billionth time, that I was really IS. Then I could just teach her to Flick! And she would be OK, no matter what her father said.

Then I saw something out of the corner of my eye.

I was right! Marco *was* down the hall. And now he was . . . heading this way!

"OMG, I think Marco Vega is coming over here," I whispered to Lindsay. I hadn't seen him since I'd gotten back.

Lindsay bit her lip. "Oh. Good luck."

"You're back from L.A.!" Marco said to me. "I saw you on the Teen Yes Awards, dude, and . . ."

AND???!!!! And what?!!!

I looked nice? I looked great? I looked stunningly beautiful and captured the heartbreaking beauty from the poem he wrote??

"And . . . you know, when the camera was on you, you could see a little bit of The Rock's face!" he said all excitedly.

Okay, righty then.

"Yeah," I said. "He was sitting in the row behind me."

"Whoa, you were sitting by The Rock. Dude!"

We walked for a little ways. I could see people looking at us. I kept one eye out for Sawyer or a Jennifer just in case.

"Well, I got math now," Marco said. "So I'll catch you—"

We walked around a corner and *bam!*

I crashed right into a sophomore guy. I got knocked almost right over . . . but Marco caught me.

"Hey!" Marco yelled at the guy. "Watch where you're going!"

"Are you OK?" Marco asked me.

I was okay now. More than okay. Marco was holding on to my arms and looking into my eyes, worried about me.

"I'll be OK. I better get to class," I said all shaky, and took off down the hall. I ran around the corner. I clutched my heart, and fell against the lockers.

$\sim$

"You won't believe the dirt I found out," the Gossipor was saying. **"Totally juicy, totally embarrassing—"** But before she could spill her evil secrets, she felt a hand on her shoulder. She turned around and gasped. IS! FLICK! The Gossipor's mouth was superglued shut forever!

IS
☆ THE SEQUEL ☆
By Jameson Bartlett

~

Leslie had asked me how I felt about writing a sequel to *IS*. Denise asked me how I felt about writing a sequel to *IS*. My dad mentioned that my new laptop would make writing a sequel to *IS* really easy. Gallagher said she'd be happy to add on a sequel to *IS* as extra credit for English class.

But no pressure, they all said. No pressure.

So I decided to see how I felt about writing a sequel to *IS*. But Kimberlee's words kept ringing in my ears. "Well, the author's fourteen. What does she know?"

And that's how I was feeling. What did I know? So how was my sequel coming?

IS: The Sequel

By Jameson Bartlett

That's as far as I'd gotten.

I couldn't write a sequel and I knew it. I could barely write something decent for school.

We had these writing critiques in English class. My group was me, Connor, Jennifer2, and Tirrell Nelson. Rats, no Marco. I looked around at everyone rearranging their desks to get into groups. Marco and Sawyer weren't in the same group. That was something.

Tirrell Nelson filled me in. "Gallagher told us to share our homework assignment with the group. And then we would all tell what we liked and didn't like about it."

I'd whipped mine off on my laptop on the flight home from California. We were supposed to write a short story with a conflict. I made sure I didn't accidentally turn in my journal this time.

Tirrell read his first. It was about two guys at a football game. One guy had dissed the other guy, and they got into a brawl. Body parts flew and then they both died slow, painful deaths. Gallagher had told us to be constructive with our criticism. So we couldn't say, like, that sucked.

"I liked how you described the setting, with the stadium and everything," Connor said generously.

"And how the guy's girlfriend was really mad at him when he insulted the other team," Jennifer2 added. "That was pretty funny."

I was having a hard time thinking of a compliment.

"I liked the uniform colors, black and red," I said. OK, I know, not a brilliant response. Connor looked at me kind of funny. Then he started talking about how Tirrell should be less graphic and have more of a plot.

Connor read his. It was good. It was about a guy who was climbing a mountain and suddenly got caught by an avalanche. We all told him we liked it.

"I liked the way he dug himself out, finger by finger," Jennifer2 told him. "You were very descriptive."

"It was the whole man versus nature conflict Gallagher told us about!" I said, triumphantly. "That was great the way he almost gave up but he found his inner strength to go on." That was better. I didn't sound like an idiot.

"I liked when you said he was going to chew his own fingers to survive," Tirrell said. "Too cool." Then we suggested Connor change some parts around. And then it was my turn.

I cleared my throat. I read my story out loud, nervously. I waited for the critique.

"It was a little, well, superficial," Jennifer2 said. "There wasn't really a whole lot of feeling in it."

"It kinda seemed like you just whipped it off to get it over with. Maybe next time you could put in a character who is likable," Connor suggested. "So we have someone to root for in the conflict. OK, Jennifer, how about your story?"

I slumped down in my seat. That was it? Is that the way to treat a bestselling author? I mean, come on. This was worse than when I went on Amazon.com and saw that someone had given me only two stars on my book review. "Overrated," Anonymous wrote. Let's see *her* try to write a book.

Whatever. I half-listened to Jennifer2's story about a girl

whose parents never listened to what she had to say because they were always arguing with each other.

"Hey, that was really good!" Connor said when Jennifer2 was done. "You really captured your character's feelings!"

"Yeah, I liked when the girl said she wanted to open her soul but her parents wouldn't close their mouths!" Tirrell told her. "Really cool." They looked at me.

"Um, it was a good example of a three-way conflict," I said lamely. Connor looked at me for a second. Then he went back to getting all excited over Jennifer2's story. Connor and Jennifer2 were all smiling at each other and going over some *minor* changes she could make.

I watched them all together and OK, yes, I was a *little* jealous of how Connor got all excited about Jennifer's story. I was noticing Connor. How he was easy to talk to. How he was really good at giving compliments to girls. But not like "nice butt" or anything like that. And how he was looking pretty cute in his green shirt with his hair flopping in his face. He wasn't really supercute but when you got to know him, he got cuter.

But oh well, he was obviously into Jennifer2. Anyway, Connor was nice and all but come on—I was getting closer to Operation Marco the Man of My Dreams Vega. I needed to keep my focus here. And like I would set myself up to try to snag both Sawyer's AND Jennifer2's guys? I DON'T think so. Now *that* would be a three-way conflict I would lose.

I walked out of English in a bad mood. I went to my locker. A couple of cheerleaders were at their lockers talking.

"Did you hear what happened to her at the Teen Yes Awards? Sawyer said that her dress was so cheap that it ripped down the back. You can't tell because they only showed her face on TV, but it was way embarrassing."

I pretended I didn't hear them. Go ahead, talk about me behind my back. What do I care. I shoved my books in my locker.

"Rrrrip! Right down the back! Can you imagine? Wouldn't you just die if you were her?" I heard one of them say as they walked away, laughing.

OK, I cared. Couldn't I do anything without Sawyer butting in and ruining it?!! I was seriously sick of Sawyer and her friends and her gossip and her lies. I thought about what Kimberlee said. She was right, we never win out against the Myrnas of the world. Because they play dirty.

25

Game Show Host: OK, contestants! Here's the Final
Question for all the money! If you answer this, you will
be the winner of Who Wants to Be a Billionaire. . . .

**What does the book character IS
do to overcome evil villains?**

A. High-fives
B. Snickers
C. Laughs
D. Flicks

I was on the phone with Harmony and signing on to check
my email as she was telling me about how she went to the
movies with Gabriela and Gabriela's friend Raj. Gabriela
had told her that she thought Harmony and Raj would be
good together. And Harmony was thinking she was right.

"He's so sweet," Harmony was saying. "He let me pick the movie and then didn't even complain afterward that it was too girly! And then we all talked for hours. He's *such* a good listener!"

"Uh-huh," I said. I went to Amazon.com to check my book rankings. Number two! I was only number two today? That wizard boy and his new book. Argh!

"And he walked each of us home. He's such a total gentleman!" Harmony said. "Jamie, this guy has potential!"

"Cool," I said, scrolling down my in-box. "Hey! I got an email from Cadyn Christopher! Hold on while I read it. . . . She's telling me about this new miniseries she got a part in. Ooh, she's going to costar with Tanner Brody!"

"Jamie," Harmony said in an annoyed way.

"What? You love Tanner Brody. You think he's a major doll baby," I said.

"Well, you are obviously preoccupied," Harmony said. "I have to go meet Gabriela anyway. So I'll catch you later."

We hung up. OK, I guess I was too distracted there. Maybe Kimberlee and her friend were two-faced. But at least Cadyn wasn't lying when she said she would email me. I'll call Harmony back later and apologize and promise to listen more. And maybe sometime I can take her to meet Tanner Brody to make it up to her. I emailed Cadyn about Marco and how he was even hotter than Ryder Donovan.

The phone was ringing.

"Hello?" I could no longer say "Bartlett Residence" because what if one of my fans had tracked down our new unlisted phone number and was stalking me or something?

"Is this Jamie?" a guy's voice asked.

"Who is this please?"

"Marco Vega."

I almost dropped the phone. MARCO VEGA! MARCO VEGA! I started hopping up and down.

"Um, hi, Marco. I'm doing well thank you. How are you?" That was totally dorky. I would have to stop that.

"Cool. I got your number from your friend Lindsay. Hope that's OK," he said.

OK? Hmm, let's see . . . was that OK? IT WAS AMAZING!!! Thank you, Lindsay!!!!

"I wanted to see if you were doing anything Friday," he said. "Or if you wanted to do something, you know. With me."

MARCO VEGA WAS ASKING ME OUT ON A DATE!!!!!!!! MARCO VEGA WAS ASKING ME OUT ON A DATE!!!!!!!!

!!!!!!!!!!!!!!

!!!!!!!!!!!!!!!!!!!

!!!!!!!!!!!!!!!!!!!!!!!!

"Jamie? You there?" Marco was saying.

"Oh, of course! Well, let me check my schedule for Friday." I put down the phone and jumped around the kitchen. I picked up the phone and used my Diana-trained voice.

"I had a cancellation Friday. So I would be free."

"How about you meet me at the mall, like six? We can grab cheese fries or something," Marco said.

"OK, yeah. See you in school." We hung up.

Then I called Harmony but got her voice mail. Oh yeah, she was out with What's-her-face. I left a message about how Marco had asked me out on a date. Woo-hoo!!!!

Mom walked in while I was dancing around.

"Oh good, are you back up to number one?" she asked me. "I saw the Amazon.com rankings today."

"No, I just got—" Wait, Jamie, hold your tongue. "I was just practicing something for gym class. We're doing interpretive dance," I finished lamely. Shoot. I forgot the whole Marco-Vega-as-Fonzie Mom and Dad problem. They weren't going to let me go out with Marco Vega. I knew it. What to do, what to do?

I was stuck in an inner conflict. I mean, it was my life's dream to go out with Marco Vega. My parents wouldn't stop me from that, would they? Yes, they would. My parents were pretty strict. They would never understand. Much as I hated to do it, I'd have to. I was on a mission. The target: Allie.

I walked into my sister's room after one really quick knock. Allie was practicing her smile in the mirror. He he. She tossed her hair around a little. Pursed her lips.

"Trying to teach yourself how to smile?" I asked her.

"Don't you know how to knock, Hollywood?" she snarled. "I'll give you five seconds to tell me why you are in my room. And then you are out."

"Well, Big Sister, I was unpacking my suitcase and I found these. They must have fallen out of my Teen Yes goodie bag," I lied. I pulled out the sunglasses I'd gotten in Hollywood. "I mean they're RayZ and all, so they are really in style. And expensive. But I just don't think they look good on me," I said. Actually I thought they did. I was prepared to make the sacrifice. I had backup if I needed it: The Ryder Donovan autograph. But I might need that for future Marco Vega dates. If there *were* any, of course.

"So, those sunglasses look like crap on you," Allie said suspiciously. "What doesn't? And your point is . . . ?"

"They might look good on you. . . . ," I said. "If you get Duh . . . g, *Doug,* to drive me to the mall Friday and pick me up, too."

"What? Why would Doug and I give up a Friday to drive you around?" she said.

"You would *not* have to give it up, you'd just have to do a little extra driving to drop me off and pick me up," I said. "Wearing your new RayZ. . . ."

"Why can't you ask Mom? She'll do anything for her precious little author these days," Allie said.

"Um, I just don't want her to say she has to do some shopping. And then try to come in and hang out with me or something. You know, so not cool," I said.

"Yeah, right. You don't want Mom to know who you are going with. I get it. Little Miss Perfect, all sneaky sneaky. Who is it, the president of the chess club?" Allie said. "Let me see those glasses." I tossed them to her. She put them on and checked herself out in the mirror. I was sorry to see them go, but Marco was worth it. . . .

"Well, all right," she said. "But you are to sit in the back-seat and not say *one word*. And I'm keeping the RayZ even if your date stands you up!"

Mission accomplished.

26

"I. Have. A. Date. With. Marco. Vega. Friday. Night. AHH-HHH!!!!!" I told Harmony, as soon as I was sure Mom had left for the grocery store and Allie wasn't within eavesdropping distance.

"I have a date with Raj Friday night!!!" Harmony told me back. And we screamed together. "AHHH!"

And then I realized something. Oh sure, it seems obvious to you. But with all this stuff going on, my mind has been kind of overloaded lately. I never really asked Harmony about this Raj guy. So.

"All right," I said generously. "You go first. Tell me all about Raj. Details."

"He's so great, Jamie," Harmony said. "He wants to be a doctor and practice in the areas of the city nobody wants to go. He's incredibly smart. Last time he went to the movies with Gab and me, we all talked for so long, like about our dreams and our goals in life. I felt like I could tell him anything. He totally respects my opinion. And his eyes are to DIE for. He's going to pick me up here, take me to a film festival, and then out to his favorite restaurant for sushi. I don't want to jinx it or anything but I think he really likes me, too."

Wow.

"Wow," I said. "He sounds perfect for you."

"Can you believe it? OK, your turn. Marco Vega! Tell me about *your* date!"

Hm. Meeting Marco at the mall for cheese fries just didn't seem to stack up in comparison to Harmony's Dream Date. But maybe we would read romantic poetry to each other, like that day in English class. Maybe he'd even write a love poem for me!

"Know what? I'm sure I'll have tons more to tell you after I get to know him better," I said. "But I definitely need your help. What am I going to wear?!?!"

Because I'm so sure you would rather hear about my BIG DATE with Marco, I'll skip ahead through the rest of the week's events. Skip over the interviews and stuff I did for the magazines and newspapers and all that. I'm slowly sort of, kind of getting used to people asking me questions, and I almost always remember to politely ask the photographers not to take the pictures from the infamous Nose angle.

Allie and Duh dropped me off at the entrance of the mall. Allie was wearing her new shades. I was wearing a jean jacket, my fave pants, and little dangly earrings. I had my black

Teen Yes tank top under my jacket, for extra coolness. I took a deep breath and walked into the food court.

Marco was already there. He was kind of hanging over the railing.

"Hey!" he spotted me and came over. "'Sup?"

"Um, not much," I said. We walked around a little bit. I tried to walk really fast when we passed Victoria's Secret. The whole window was half-naked Amber Tiffany.

"I met her at the after-party. She was pretty boring," I said. "Amber Tiffany, I mean."

"Who cares! With a bod like that!" Marco replied.

Ookay, let's change that subject.

"Are you hungry?" I asked him. He nodded and we went back to the food court. He got two double hamburgers, a chicken sandwich, super fries, and a soda. I got diet soda and cheese fries. I hated eating in front of guys. What if something dribbled down my face or something? But cheese fries was "our" food. He paid for my meal, too. He insisted!

"Want some cheese fries?" I asked him, hoping to spark that common interest. Like we had shared at the cafeteria.

"Naw, got my own fries. Thanks," he said.

We sat in silence. Doo doo doo. OK, what could I say? I thought about Harmony and Raj on their date right now, discussing their mutual interests and goals for the future.

I didn't know of our *mutual* interests. But I'd been preparing for this moment, reading up on cars on the Internet!

"Hey, so you like Maserati Spyders?" I said.

"Yeah!" That perked him right up. He talked about all the different features the car had. I stared at his mouth while he was talking. His mouth was so perfect. His black hair was so shiny. He was so HOT. Hot hot hottie. And he was sitting across from me. Sigh.

"So do you think you'll get one?" Marco was saying.

"Uh . . . Get one what?" I forgot that he was talking. I was too busy looking.

"A spider!"

"Where, where, where? . . . Is it on me??!" I jumped up and almost knocked over the fries. I hate spiders.

"No—a Maserati Spyder. I mean, with the money from your book?"

Oops. I sat down quickly. All righty. So oh, was he after my money? Is that why he asked me out? A gold digger?

"No," I said. "My parents are putting all that money away in the bank. Like for college and stuff. I did get to give some of my money to some charities, though."

"Bummer," he said. I'm sure he meant no Maserati Spyder, not the charity part. But he didn't jump up and flee in horror. That was a relief. I never thought of someone going out with me for my money. I guess since I never had any before. And in a way, still didn't. Thanks to Mr. and Mrs. Let's-Not-Let-Money-Change-Our-Lives Bartlett.

Now would be a good time to revive that other spark between us. The poetry.

"So, what do you think of English class?" I asked him. "Do you like this year better than last year?"

"Yeah," he said. "Gallagher doesn't make us read our stuff out loud. I hated that."

Yes, he would, wouldn't he. I remembered how he said he hated sharing his poem out loud. Made sense if he was trying to conceal his love of writing poetry.

"Yeah, I remember you said that last year," I prompted him. "When we were partners. . . ."

"Were you in my English class?" he asked.

"No offense," he added, seeing my face fall.

"Yeah, you read a poem to me out loud?" I told him.

"Oh YEAH," he said, slapping his forehead. "I remember that. Man, that was way embarrassing. I had to block that out of my memory."

Aw, that was sweet. He was embarrassed about reading the poem to me. I felt a little better.

"I'm done," Marco said, finishing his burger. "Wanna go check out some posters?" We headed over to the poster store. I waved a little "hi" to Cadyn on the *Brentley Street* poster.

It was almost time for Allie to pick me up.

"I guess we better go," I said. "My ride will be here soon." We walked in silence to the main entrance. I thanked Marco for inviting me. We stood there and, oh yeah, oh yeah, he was leaning forward and

*****K-I-S-S-I-N-G*****

Me and Marco Vega were smooching by the main entrance of the mall!!!!!! *Kiss! Kiss! Kiss!*

No tongue or anything, just lip action. *Kiss! Kiss!*

Out of the corner of my eye, I saw Duh's car pull up. I

didn't want Allie to see who I was with. One thing, 'cause of her Pom Squad association with Sawyer. But also because she would have blackmail on me with my parents about dating the Fonz.

I had to break away. "I'll see you at school," I said, all breathless and Marilyn Monroe.

"I'll call you," Marco Vega said.

I bounced into the car.

"Oh look at the happy girl, home from her first date," Allie sneered. "Did you get some good chess tips?"

I gave her my best, "I'm sorry, did you say something?" look. I kept my promise not to say a word in Duh's car. I didn't want to spoil my happy mood. I leaned back and smiled, thinking about Marco Vega's lips on mine.

~

Myrna raged at her emergency meeting of the Evil Clique of Populors.

"She's taken out some of our best! They're having no effect on her at all. Her Flicks are becoming more powerful. I command you . . . IS MUST BE CRUSHED!"

27

To: Jamie
From: Oliver

I appreciate your fulfilling your radio and TV interview requests. But you still have outstanding print requests and deadlines are approaching. Please let me know when you can complete the following:

1. The essay on girls in today's society for <u>The New Yorker</u>.
2. The short story for <u>TweenScene</u>'s winter issue.
3. The short story for the anthology about high school.

Plus, you've been asked to be the teen advice columnist for the Syndicated News Service, serving more than 1,500 newspapers. If you're interested in a monthly column, let me know.

~

Yiy.

I stared at my laptop, wishing words would materialize. OK, let's start with #1. The essay on girls in today's society for *The New Yorker*.

Um. OK. I typed on my laptop. "Girls in today's society are . . . ." Hm.

"Stressed out." I continued. Yes, that was true. Too many demands on them. That was pretty IS-like.

They are stressed out *because* . . . I thought. But my mind wandered to last night. To Marco Vega kissing me. OK, focus, Jamie. Focus.

". . . because publicists are placing unrealistic demands on them to complete requests for contributions to major magazines and newspapers on top of their regular homework."

Click, click, click . . . I pressed the Delete button.

I wanted to write something good. I really did. But I knew they wanted something Super-IS from me. Pressure.

My cell phone rang.

"So. Marco Vega kissed you," Harmony said. I'd given her the scoop last night.

"Yup." I sighed. I thought about Marco's kiss . . . how he leaned over toward me. And slowly pressed his lips on mine. He tasted like fries. Regular, not cheesy.

"Marco and Jamie, sitting in a tree. K-I-S-S-I-N-G!" Harmony sang.

"Um . . . my mom is right here," I whispered. My face was red, thinking of K-I-S-S-I-N-G Marco with my mom sitting so close.

We were in the backseat of a car. Mom wasn't driving because . . . we had a driver! Because I was in New York City going to an event! And Oliver arranged for a car to pick us up. And the event was my first book signing!

Which I thought sounded pretty fun. More fun than writing essays and short stories, anyway. I clicked my laptop shut.

Harmony was going to come for moral support. Then I was going to stay the night at Harmony's mother's. Mom had come down here with me, but she was going to stay at a hotel.

The car pulled up to the bookstore.

— BOOK SIGNING —
JAMESON BARTLETT
Author of IS
Appearing today from 2:00 to 4:00 p.m.

"Ready, Jameson?" The lady who worked at the bookstore met us at the door, smiling. She led me to a table up front that had huge stacks of *IS*.

There were girls, moms, even a couple guys packed around the signing table. There was a huge line and the bookstore workers were trying to keep people in control.

"Wow!" my mom said. "This is like the Beatles!"

"Jameson!" someone screamed. Everyone was yelling *Jameson! Jameson!* OK. OK. This was a little crazy.

"James!" Whew, it was Harmony. She pushed her way through the crowd and jumped in next to me. "This is insane! What are you, Gwen Stefani?"

I got out my favorite glitter-gel pens I had brought to sign books. I picked silver and purple for today. I had been practicing my signature on my notebooks during class. "Isabella loves you!" I had tried. No, too corny. "Best wishes, Jamie Bartlett." Too dull. I finally decided on "Flick!!" and my name, decorated with Isabella's signature little stars.

The first girl came up. She was really excited. "I've been waiting outside to meet you all morning!" she said. She handed me a copy of my book she'd bought. I signed it. I smiled right at the girl, the way Diana had taught me. Individual attention.

"Whoa, good smile," Harmony whispered.

I felt a little fake for a second. I mean, Diana had to teach me to smile at people? But really, I did want them to feel good. Like they had connected with me. We had an author visit my school in sixth grade and she signed a book for me. I still remembered how she smiled at me and said, "I'm glad you liked my book." I wanted everyone to feel that way when they met me. Not that I thought meeting *me* was a big deal, but meeting an author, and all that . . .

"What's your name?" I asked her.

"Taylor," she said. "And I loved your book. Isabella meant so much to me and—"

"Thank you!" the bookstore person kind of nudged her on. I smiled at her again, feeling kind of bad she got pushed on, but what can you do? There were about 300 other people behind her. I smiled up at the next woman.

"Please sign this one for my granddaughter, Amy. If you

could write 'Gramma loves you and wants you to learn from Isabella and stay away from that Bryan character, he's bad news' . . . I would appreciate it!"

I signed books for two hours. I thought my hand was about to fall off. Everyone was so nice though. I mean, you know that feeling when you write a poem or something and have someone read it? And then they like it and they tell you it was good, and you feel all great about that? Well, that was what it was like for me. Except I had it for two hours straight! From girls, moms, dads, grandmothers. Pretty cool. But seriously exhausting.

Someone else was handing me a book. I could barely see straight.

"Could you write 'To My Very Good Friend,' please?" said a guy's voice.

"Um, well, I don't know if—" I looked up. It was Connor!

"Connor!" I jumped up. "What are you doing here?"

"My grandmother lives in the city, so I thought I'd come down and get her a personally autographed *IS*," he said.

"Wow, I'm totally surprised!" I was! And happy to see him.

"This is my grandmother. Grandma, this is Jamie." Connor introduced the woman standing next to him.

"Connor speaks so highly of you." She pressed her hand into mine. "I read your book. It was very wise."

"Um, well, I don't know everything. I mean, I don't know that I'm so wise. Sometimes I think I just channeled Isabella somehow or—"

"Jamie isn't so great at taking compliments." Connor laughed. "Say, 'Thank you,' Jamie."

"Thanks," I said, all embarrassed.

"I read online that your book just won a library association award," Connor said. "That's pretty cool."

"Yeah," I told him. "I'm excited. I still can't believe it."

"Well, isn't that wonderful. Congratulations, and it was a pleasure to meet you," his grandmother said.

"Thank you, and it was nice to meet you," I told her.

"Yeah, we'll stop clogging up your line," Connor said.

"See you in school!" I yelled to Connor. I watched him leave. He turned around and waved. I was suddenly feeling less exhausted.

The next girl in line came up to me. She seemed really nervous.

"Hi, I'm Madison," the girl said. "I'm so nervous. I haven't read your book yet. But there's this girl in my class, she's so mean to me. She's always saying stuff to me at school. My mom told me we should come get your book."

I looked at her. I wanted to help her so bad. I picked up my gel pen.

Madison —
We all need some extra Flicks sometimes.
So here's some especially for you.
From Jamie Bartlett

The bookstore person moved her along. I watched her go. I wished I could do more.

28

Later that night I was collapsed on Harmony's bed in her apartment, watching the news.

"Hundreds of girls came out today to meet Jameson Bartlett, fourteen-year-old author of the bestseller *IS*."

The camera panned over a line of girls, carrying copies of *IS*. One of them held up a sign: I CAME 200 MILES TO SEE IS!!!

"It's my favorite book ever!" some girl shrieked into the camera. "WE LOVE IS!" two other girls shouted.

Then there was a shot of me, signing books, flashing my smile at the blur of girls.

"It's great to meet all these fans," the Me on TV said into the camera. "I'm, well, overwhelmed."

"Whew, you looked tired!" Harmony said, as the news segment ended.

"I'll never be able to move my fingers again," I groaned. "By the last book, I think I was spelling my name Janie Bttt. I need to shorten my name. To like, J or something." I went through three glitter pens. I'm serious, my fingers were about to fall off.

Harmony held the slice of Hawaiian pizza up to my mouth so I could bite it. My hands were wrapped in hot wet towels.

"I can't believe Connor came to your signing. That was so cool," Harmony said. "Are you *sure* there's nothing going on with you two? Did I sense sparks?"

"No you did *not*. First of all, he's going out with Jennifer2. They're together, like, all the time. And second, hello? I had a date with Marco? Marco Vega? Remember him? The hottest, most incredible, coolest guy in our entire grade and I would go so far as to say our entire school? The guy who kissed me? And told me to call him tonight? Connor's a nice guy and The End."

Harmony stuffed more pizza in my mouth. A piece of pineapple fell on my neck. I didn't care. I was too tired to move.

"OK, I got it. So let me tell you more about Raj," Harmony said. "While I have you captive. He's sooo sweet. He brought me a flower to our date. It's so great he's homeschooled, cause he can come over sometimes in the morning to do homework. And he really studies hard! I mean, he's so focused on going premed already."

"Geez, and he doesn't even have grades to worry about," I grumbled, motioning my head for another bite of pizza.

"He says he wants to learn for the sake of learning." Harmony sighed. Finally, someone with enough brains to challenge Harmony "Prodigy" Pinckney. "I wish you could meet him tomorrow. But he's doing some math competition in the Bronx. He's so adorable."

He was. I'd seen his picture.

"I'm starting to believe you invented this perfect guy. Are you sure he's real?" I teased her.

"Oh he's so real. You will have to meet him soon. I'll get your schedules coordinated."

I can't believe my best friend in the world has a boyfriend and I have never even met him. I thought about that for a second. I used to know everything in Harmony's life. I mean, even last year when she moved down here for half the time she still had most of her social life upstate. Now she was getting this whole new life. A new boyfriend I'd never even seen except in pictures.

"Oh," Harmony interrupted my thoughts. "Gabriela's going to come over for brunch tomorrow. Did I tell you? She wants to meet you."

And a new City Best Friend.

"You'll love Gabriela. Everybody does," Harmony said. "You have to ask her about when she, Raj, and I went to Central Park and . . . well, ask her. She tells it so much better than I do."

A new funny City Best Friend *everybody* just loves who might be trying to replace me as Best Friend. Argh. Harmony was still talking about Gabriela.

"Harmony, Marco told me to call him tonight," I interrupted her. "So if you don't mind . . ."

"Oh, sure," she said. "Have a good phone call!"

I unwrapped one hand so I could dial his number. I curled up on the bed. Talking to Marco would cheer me up!

"Hey, dude," Marco said when I told him it was me. "Are you in New York City?"

"Yeah. I had a book signing today. My hands are about to fall off from signing my name so many times," I said to him.

"*Your* hands are about to fall off? Dude, let me tell you mine are, too. You should have seen what I did. I fixed my mom's carburetor today—it took forever. She's got this SUV, you should see the engine on this thing. First I had to . . ."

Myrna was furious. Her Villainesses were dropping like flies. She knew what she had to do—bring out the "B" team:

> **The Backstabbor**
> **The Betrayor**
> **The Best Friend Stealor**

~

"Jamie, Jamie!"

Harmony was shaking me. I was on a bed . . . at . . . Harmony's mom's apartment. . . . I looked down. I was still in my clothes. Something gooey was on my neck. A piece of pineapple. Gross.

"It's ten in the morning. You passed out last night on the phone with Marco!" Harmony said.

OMG! I fell asleep when I was on the phone with Marco? I mean, I was so tired. Plus, the whole carburetor engine *blah blah blah.*

"I came in and you were sleeping with the phone on your ear."

"Oh no, I hope I didn't tick off Marco!" I said. This was not the way to start a relationship!

"No, I saved you," Harmony said. "He was still talking and I just pretended to be my mom picking up on the other line saying it was late and you had to hang up. So everything's cool."

"Whew. Thanks, Harmony," I said.

"But get up! Gabriela's coming over any minute."

Harmony was already showered and dressed in a T-shirt she'd designed herself, red belt, jeans she'd patched, knee-high boots. Harmony's apartment buzzer rang.

"She's here," Harmony said. "Get ready fast. Hurry." She ran out before I could say anything.

Well, OK, Miss Bossy. I will go meet your precious friend. I threw on the only thing I'd unpacked—a gray hoodie and track pants. I ran a brush through my hair, but it was hopeless. I threw in a scrunchie and followed the sound of laughter into the kitchen.

"Jamie! It's so great to meet you!" The girl who had to be Gabriela came over and held out her hand to shake. I shook. Ugh. She was adorable. Long brown hair, black slim pants, and a black shirt. Cool choker. The casual chic look. She was bouncing to Harmony's cabinets to get a glass. She obviously knew where everything was. Made herself right at home.

"So Gabriela was just telling me how Adam—this guy we know, from Gabriela's homeschool group—was doing the funniest thing . . . ," Harmony said to me, well kind of toward me, and they both starting cracking up hysterically. Um, was anyone going to share what this funniest thing was? Apparently not.

But Gabriela stopped laughing. "No in-jokes," she warned Harmony. "We don't want Jamie to feel left out. Jamie, I want to hear all about your book signing. It must have been so exciting."

Gabriela asked me all sorts of questions like she was really interested. In the midst of it, Harmony managed to get in how Gabriela is going to be in the national spelling bee next month.

"Oh stop," Gabriela said. "Spelling's big in my house. I mean, my mom being so into books and all, as Jamie knows."

"But listen to this," Harmony said. Turns out Gabriela also got a callback for an off-Broadway show. AND wait until you see her dance, it's so amazing. Blah blah yeah whatever.

Ugh. I excused myself to go to the bathroom. I heard Harmony and Gabriela talking about double-dating with Raj and Adam, who probably looked like Brad Pitt's younger brother. It was the Attack of the Genius, Beautiful and Perfect People. I felt sick. I tried to picture me and Marco coming along on a triple date but couldn't quite do it.

I looked at myself in the mirror. Oh great. I hadn't removed the damn pineapple. I could just hear Gabriela talking to her friends. "Jameson Bartlett? She was kind of quiet and weird. And she had this pineapple sticking to her the whole time and what was I supposed to do, say to a best-selling author, 'Excuse me, but you have pineapple sticking to your neck'?" Then they'd all laugh.

Speaking of laughing, Harmony and Gabriela were at it again. They needed to stop that.

I went to Harmony's bedroom and opened my laptop to check email. An email from Cadyn Christopher! Well, Harmony isn't the only one with a cool new friend. So there. I read the email:

```
Sup! Your book signing sounds awesome!
:) Shooting ended early today so we're
hitting the beach! G2G! Cadyn.
```

Well, that was not fulfilling.

There was a new email from Altan8, the girl who had written before about her rotten friends and parents.

```
Well, things are getting worse. I asked
this guy to go out with me. And he said
no, let's just be friends. I'm a LOSER.
The only guys who are interested in me
are in chat rooms. And that's because
they don't have to look at me in per-
son. I gained four pounds. I could die.
Please write back. I could use a dose
of IS right now. C Ya.
```

What could I say? I didn't know. I hit Save. I didn't feel much like an empowered advice giver at the moment. I definitely couldn't give her any IS now. I needed it for myself! Someone was stealing my BFF right out from under me. I was being Sawyered. I was seeing, kind of, my dream guy, so that should be good, right? But even the thought of Marco wasn't cheering me up.

I lay down on Harmony's bed.

I blinked back some tears. Harmony and her *new* best friend didn't seem to notice I hadn't come back. Shouldn't they both be a little more excited to hang out with ME? I mean, it is MY manuscript that Gabriela told her mother she loved so much.

This sucks. Sucks, sucks, sucks. I picked up my cell to see if Mom would pick me up early. I wanted to go home.

1220 WFLI Talk-Radio Show Guests:

9:00 a.m.:   Biological warfare expert Eli Rossi, M.D.

10:30 a.m.:   Secondary education expert
Dr. Dawn Welch

11:00 a.m.:   Author Jameson Bartlett

The weirdest thing about doing radio interviews is that most of the time you don't even have to be in the studio. You don't have to even be in the same state. You can be sitting at home in your pj's, gabbing away on your own phone. Except instead of talking to your BFF you're talking with some talk-radio person. Like right now, my voice is being broadcast through a radio station in some state I can barely locate on a map.

"Our guest today on *Talk 1220* in Sioux Falls is Jameson Bartlett, author of the bestseller *IS*," announced the host guy from his radio booth.

"Hi, Sioux Falls. Please, call me Jamie," I said dutifully.

"Jamie, for the one or two listeners who haven't read your book, tell us about it."

I recited the answer Diana had practiced with me, while determining that the silver gel pen definitely looked better with my skin color than gold.

"Well, Jamie, isn't it true that on page twenty-two, your character feels inferior because of reading magazines?"

"Um, sort of—" I said, drawing *Jamie Bartlett Vega* . . . *Marco + Jamie TLA* on my hand in silver.

"How, then, do you justify the fact that your book is being featured in virtually every teen magazine in the country this month, contributing to your sales and your profits?" the radio guy continued. "And that advertisements promoting your book can be found in two of the three leading teen magazines this month alone?"

"Um, wait. It's not that the magazines are bad. What happens is that IS shows how it's *some* of the stuff in *some* of the magazines, and then, like, how you *react* to stuff and, um, how our society is . . ." OK, I was babbling.

Argh—Diana, where are you when I need you?!!!

"Do you read teen magazines yourself, Jamie?" DJ Jerk asked.

"Yeah, I do, but what I'm trying to say is . . ."

"You heard it here, Jamie Bartlett *does* read teen magazines. It's time to cut to a commercial, folks! Let's see what our listeners have to say . . . right after the break!"

"Jamie, hold on for three minutes of commercials, then we'll be back on with you."

OK, I'm on hold. Quick! Help! I looked around for Diana's Client EmUrgency Hotline number. Where was it, where was it? . . .

I know, I know. Diana has trained me for these situations, but it's really hard. What would happen if I just said, Look, I'm fourteen years old and I'm not an expert in any of this! You think I really know the answer to this?

But then the other part of me is like, Wow, I get to make a huge impact on all of these girls my age. I have to be a role model, like IS. I have to inspire them.

The problem was, I *didn't* have all the answers. I mean, I created IS, but I could make things however I wanted in my book.

Yes, my book was advertised in teen magazines. Yes, I read teen magazines. I *like* to read teen magazines. Now I'm trying to read them the Isabella way. At least I was ripping out stuff that made me feel bad, or skipping right past it. Honest. I was improving.

Bliiing! My cell phone was ringing. Great. Maybe it was Diana and I could ask her how to handle this!

"Jamie?" Oh, it was Lindsay. "I couldn't get through to your other line. I really need your advice on something."

OH NO! Not more advice! I can't do it anymore. I am not a walking advice column, OK? I am Jamie Bartlett, regular girl. Yeah, I wrote a book in which every girl's problems were fixed. But guess what?

IT'S FICTION! THERE'S NO SUCH THING AS IS!!!!

"Lindsay!" I said in a big burst. "I CAN'T help you. I have to get back to the other line. I'm on hold and . . ."

"Well, FINE!" Lindsay snapped, suddenly not sounding like Lindsay. "What, is Cadyn Christopher on the other line? Marco Vega? HARMONY? One of your more important friends? I am *always* here for you. I listen to you *Marco Marco Marco* all the time. I even went to the Popular Table with you while everyone ignored me. And you know what, I'm tired of being blown off by you. Like I'm a NOTHING. You're acting . . . you're acting . . . like Myrna!"

Click. Lindsay hung up on me.

On my other phone, I heard the radio-show jingle music come back on. The radio guy was back in my receiver. "Welcome back to *Talk 1220*! We're chatting with Jamie Bartlett, bestselling author of *IS*.

"We're running out of time, so let's just move on to our first caller!" the radio guy said. (Whew.) "Hellooo, Ashley, you're on with Jamie."

"Am I really talking to Jamie? Jamie, I am so your biggest fan. I'm on my cell, and guess what? I'm camped out in front of the radio station waiting for you to come out! I have been waiting here for hours. This is the biggest moment of my life!!"

31

I felt bad that Ashley was camping out at the radio station waiting for me. I was home in NY in my pajamas. I was feeling pretty bummed out for me, too. Things were spinning out of control. But so many great things were happening to me with my book, and who was going to throw *me* a pity party?

Certainly not Harmony, with her new BFF and her new SuperBoyfriend.

Harmony *had* called me after I got back upstate. It didn't go well.

"Hey, what was your deal today?" she'd said.

"Nothing, I felt sick," I muttered.

"Look, Jamie," Harmony said. "You were pretty rude to Gabriela today. She was all excited to meet you and now I can't imagine what she's thinking."

"I know what she's thinking," I said, ticked off that Harmony was ticked off at me. "She's thinking: Oh Jamie Bartlett is such a disappointment. I thought I was meeting IS, and she's not IS. I know it, you know it . . ."

"Hey, wait a minute. All you've been doing lately is sitting around and whining that you're not IS. Sitting around wishing you were like IS," Harmony said to me. "Get up and do something about it, Jamie. You don't get to be like IS just by flicking your hand around, do you?"

"Harmony . . . ," I said. Uh-oh. She sounded really mad.

"Look, Jamie. I know you're dealing with a lot, OK? We can talk later. Right now it's not a good time," she said. "I gotta go."

She hung up.

Harmony went off on me. Lindsay called me a Myrna.

I needed some emotional support. Some cheering up. Something.

I called Marco.

"Hey dude, what's up?" he said.

"Not much, just hanging out."

"Well, yeah. So I'm watching the wrestling and then you can't believe what happened." And then there were twenty minutes of world wrestling. And twenty minutes of the features of the new Porsche, which wasn't as good as the Spyder in his eyes but he wouldn't turn it down if someone gave it to him. And on and on . . .

I didn't like wrestling. Or cars. Just cheese fries. All we had in common was . . . cheese fries. And the whole poetry thing . . . the love of literature . . . what happened to that?

I thought about our date at the mall. I had yet to have one decent conversation with the guy. And I'd been blaming myself. I was too nervous to talk, I kept telling myself. But it takes two to make conversation, doesn't it? Shouldn't Marco say something like, "How was *your* day, Jamie?" or "What do *you* like to do?" or "How is your book?" or something, *anything?*

I needed to get some kind of connection here! Where was the Marco who wrote beautiful love poems??

"And the hubcaps? Awesome," Marco was saying.

"Hey, Marco," I said, interrupting him. This was my last chance. I needed to unleash the Marco I had first fallen for.

"Remember that day we were partners in English class last year? When you read that poem we got assigned for homework? About the sunsets and true love and all that?"

"Oh yeah," Marco said. "Dude, that was bad."

"What?"

"Man, I was so busted. Got a week's detention for that one." Marco groaned.

"What are you talking about?" I asked him.

"That poem I bought off Tyler Jones?" Marco said. "Mr. Bleemos was so pissed, man. He's all, 'Plagiarizing can get you expelled, Mr. Vega.' And I'm like, well, *dude*, you assigned a poem. Like what, I'M supposed to *write* a poem? How was I supposed to know Tyler would sell me some *famous* poem?"

Oh.

Marco Vega had bought the poem off Tyler Jones. Who got it from the Internet.

That was it. I had to face it. Marco + Jamie was not a relationship IS fans would be cheering on.

It wasn't like he was mean or anything. But I couldn't be hoping every other girl in the universe was going to be more like Isabella and then wimp out myself. I know, I know. No Guy is better than Wrong Guy. Marco Vega = Wrong Guy. Hot Mama Guy. Good Kissing Guy. But definitely Wrong Guy for me.

Good-bye, Marco. I told him I had to go and hung up. I wasn't in the mood right now to tell him my Good-bye was really *Good-bye*.

32

So there I was. All alone. Very, very alone. This really sucked. Suddenly my laptop announced "You've got mail!"

It was from Altan8. I felt even worse. I'd totally neglected her—I never wrote her back after she was practically begging for attention. Maybe I'd read it later, I wasn't in the mood to feel sorry for anyone else but me. But I clicked on Read.

Dear Jamie,
I know you're really busy getting back from NYC and everything. But I've got a plan I wanted to tell you about so you could maybe send some IS thoughts my way so it all goes OK.

Here it is: I've been emailing with this guy I met in a chat room, he's really kewl. His parents are divorced and they were always fighting so he

knows what I'm going thru. He lives in
San Francisco and he wants me to go out
there and meet him. He knows I'm only
15 but it's ok with him even tho he's
28 since I'm really mature for my age.
I really need someone who cares about
me, you know? And he's there for me.
So I'm going to do it. I'm going to the
bus station in a little bit and by the
time my parents even notice I'll be way
gone. I won't have a computer so I just
wanted to say bye to you and thanks for
listening.

WHAT?!

Altan8 was going to take a bus across country to meet
some older guy she met in a chat room!?! She's like my age
and OMG! He could be some pervert! Or worse!

I had to stop her. I had to stop her!!!!!!

ISFlix: Altan8 R U THERE?

I IM'ed her as fast as I could. I waited. Please be there,
please be there, I was praying. Come on, come on, answer
me.

Dling.

Altan8: Jamie? Is that really u?

YES! She hadn't left yet.

ISFlix: I got your message! I just don't think it's such a great idea.
Altan8: You don't understand. Once I get to San Fran then Chet said I could crash with him. So I have a place to stay.

Not good. Think, Jamie, think.

Altan8: GG, the bus is at 6.
ISFlix: Wait!

Wait, what? . . .

ISFlix: I wanted to tell u u won a live chat with me and some prizes. For being a #1 fan!! Congratulations!!!

I needed to stall her. What could I do? What could I do?! I needed help.

Altan8: Really? I never won ne thing be4 in my life! !!!

Maybe I could make her put her mother on or something!

(172)

**ISFlix: Yeah! You won! R yr parents there to
sign for the permission?
Altan8: No, they r out.**

I ran to Allie's bedroom and banged on the door.

"Allie! Get Mom!" I yelled at her. "Get Dad!"

"Mom and Dad are at Home Depot, getting shelves to put your awards on, Creep. So go away!" Allie yelled back.

I busted in. For the first time, I appreciated Mom and Dad's No-Locking-Bedroom-Doors policy. Allie was lying on her bed. She sat up.

"Get out of here," she snarled.

"Allie—I need you. Really need you. Please," I begged.

"I said, OUT." She didn't even look up.

"Allie . . . this is serious. RETSIS, Allie! RETSIS!" I said the code word from our childhood, the word to stop our fights. OK, it was pretty stupid. But I didn't know how else to tell her I needed her.

She looked up at me.

"This better be really, really important," she said.

"It is, I promise." I rushed on before she changed her mind. "I don't know what to do. There's this girl emailing me and she says she's going to run off to be with some twenty-eight-year-old guy she met in a chat room. She's saying she's going to catch a bus to San Francisco and she's leaving NOW!"

Allie jumped off her bed.

"Show me."

The IM conversation was still on the screen.

"Are you sure she's for real? What if it's some forty-year-old guy pretending to be a girl to get your sympathy?" Allie asked, reading the screen.

"I think she's for real. I followed all the rules from that Internet Safety class Mom and Dad made us take. She's emailed me a bunch of times before," I said.

"Show me the old emails," Allie instructed.

"OK," I said. "Go to the folder called, um, TheyLoveMe."

"Oooookay. Quick, IM the girl again and stall her some more while I turn on the other computer," Allie said. "I'm going to read her other emails and see if I can get some clues."

"Clues to what?" I asked her.

"Just do it, we don't have much time."

ISFlix: You still there?

Altan8: Leaving soon.

ISFlix: I'm sorry about your parents.

Altan8: Yeah, it really sux.

ISFlix: They fight all the time?

Altan8: Yeah. But they pretend to be all fine outside the house. My friends don't even know they're fighting! I have 2 make things look perfect all the time.

ISFlix: UR right. That sux.

"Bam! Got something!" Allie ran back in. "OK, tracked down that she's actually here in town. Maybe I can trace her further . . . let me look at your computer a second."

Huh?

"Let me try tapping into this network . . . ," Allie said, typing furiously. "OK, password, loading, loading, good, good, search . . . come on, faster . . ."

Was this my sister?

"Who is she, who is she?" Allie was muttering to herself, scrolling through IM. "OK, you told her you were in New York visiting Harmony, what else did you say to her lately?"

"I didn't tell her I was in the city," I said. "I haven't emailed her in weeks." I was feeling really guilty about that. I just never felt in the mood for someone else's problems, I was so wrapped up in my own.

"Well then how did she know that you just got back upstate?" Allie demanded. "See, in her IM, she knew you just got back from the city."

Wait a minute. How did Altan8 know that? It wasn't in the papers or on my fan site or anything. I'd never mentioned my own personal life to her, I was positive. Internet Safety Rule #1: Don't give out any personal information online. I followed the rules obsessively not only because of the whole safety thing, but also because I knew my parents would yank the plug on my new laptop if I didn't.

"Come on, Jamie. You've got to know more about her. I mean, you told her your home email so you guys must share some info, right?" Allie said.

"She doesn't have my home email," I said. "Just my ISFlix."

"Yes she does, she's emailed you on your JustMe screen name before. See?" Allie brought up my Old Mail. She was right.

"How'd she get that?" I said. "I only give that out to my friends and, like, the school directory. Nothing related to IS, though."

Wait a minute. School directory. And Altan8 knew I was visiting Harmony in New York. Wait a minute. Someone at school?!!!

Something was nagging at me. OK, what was it about Altan8 I was missing here? I thought about her emails. Someone whose parents were fighting all the time and wouldn't listen to her. Someone who didn't make the cheer-leading squad.

"Allie!" I screamed. "It's Jennifer2! She wrote a story about her parents fighting for our writing critique group! She didn't make the cheerleading squad like Sawyer and Jennifer1. She's the substitute. The ALTERNATE. Get it? ALTA-N-eight! It's got to be Jennifer2! I mean, Jennifer Roth!"

Allie jumped up. "OK! Should we call the police? Are her parents home?"

"No," I said. "She said they were out."

Allie clicked on more keys. "OK. I got her address. I'll track down Mom."

"And I'll go over there," I said.

She lived a couple streets over from Harmony. I biked as fast as I could. I had no idea what I was going to do when I got there. But I had to get there.

I got to Jennifer2's house. I rang the bell. I rang it again.

Answer it, Jennifer, answer it.

Jennifer came to the door.

"Jamie! What are you doing here?"

"Um, congratulations? I'm here for that live chat you won?" I said to her, with a big fake smile. "It meant a really LIVE chat, live and in person!"

"How did you know that was me! Wait! You can't just come over to my house, I mean—" She was all confused.

"Hey, look, is this the way my fan is supposed to treat me?" I said. "Aren't you going to invite me in?"

She let me in the door, reluctantly. Jennifer looked all stressed out. She was chewing her nails, obviously not happy to see me.

"Jennifer, OK, we need to talk. It really sucks about your parents and your friends and cheerleading and all that. I know how Sawyer and the other Jennifer can be."

She turned red. "Don't tell Sawyer I said any of that stuff. I mean, you aren't supposed to know that was me emailing you."

"I won't say anything," I said. "But look, you can't run off to San Francisco. You just *can't*. It's not safe! You don't know this guy! He could be dangerous!"

"I know Chet would never do anything to hurt me."

"OK, but Jennifer! A girl traveling alone? That's not

safe! Think about everything you hear on the news! You CAN'T go!"

Jennifer stood up.

"I *am* going," she said. "Chet is waiting for me. You can't stop me. I know you're IS, but you still can't stop me from going."

She pushed past me. She started to go upstairs.

I sank down on a couch.

"You're right about one thing. And you're way wrong about another," I called up to her. "You're right I can't stop you. But you're wrong if you think I'm IS. I'm nothing like IS."

"What are you talking about?" she said. "You're Jameson Bartlett, Bestselling Author. You're IS."

"No, I'm not IS," I said. And it all came out in a rush. "I mean, you see me at school. Do I seem like IS? If I were IS I'd be able to fix my own problems. Yeah right. My life is totally crashing down on me. I mean, it's nothing awful like your parents. But remember how you emailed me that your friends were leaving you out of everything? I was just visiting Harmony and she found a new best friend and they were all talking and leaving me out and they didn't even notice I was gone. Then even Lindsay told me off! OK, and my sister makes me crazy! Then this guy I crushed on . . . *so* didn't work out."

And Sawyer makes my life miserable on a daily basis. But I didn't say that out loud.

"Wow." Jennifer came over and sat down on the couch next to me. "Wow."

"See?" I said. "So I can't stop you from going. I can't even figure out how to do the right thing half the time myself. I can't even talk to anyone about all this!!!"

"Why not?"

"Because everybody expects me to be IS and I am sooooo not! I mean, I don't know what to do myself half the time. But it's not like I can tell anyone that! And say what? Guess what, Flickers? I'm a FRAUD!!!"

I burst into tears. Next thing you know I'm crying all over the place. I could tell Jennifer didn't know what to do. She gave me an awkward little hug.

And then all of a sudden, the door burst open. And it was Allie. And my mom!

"Hey!" Jennifer yelled, jumping up and glaring at me. "You didn't mean any of that! You were just tricking me to stall me!"

"I wish I was!" My tears kept coming.

"Jamie?" my mom said, all worried. "Are you OK? Jennifer? Are you OK? What is going on here?!"

"Allie, Mom," I said. "It's OK, it's OK. Can you wait a minute? I just need to talk to Jennifer alone."

My mom started to protest, but Allie stopped her.

"We can guard the door, Mom," Allie said.

I turned to Jennifer.

"I *wish* I was just saying all that to stall you," I said. "But it's totally true. And it sucks. Everything sucks."

Jennifer looked at me. "Yeah," she sighed. "Things really suck."

I kind of smiled.

"I can't believe I cried all over you. Don't tell anyone I did that, OK? Way embarrassing. Or what I said, OK? I didn't mean to tell anybody that stuff."

"You should probably tell somebody. You know what IS says, the whole 'share your feelings and don't keep them inside.' I don't want you to go over the edge or anything, you know? I *am* one of your biggest fans," Jennifer said. "Plus, I'm waiting for a sequel."

"Ack." I smiled. "Don't even go there."

"Maybe your mom can help you? Unless she's like my mom . . ." Jennifer's voice trailed off. We looked at my mom.

I had a thought. A kind of dorky thought but . . . "Yeah, I guess I can talk to her," I said. "And, um, maybe you should, too? She does write this advice thing for the paper." OK, it was on gardening. But still.

Jennifer didn't say anything for a minute. She looked really, really tired. Then she nodded.

We went over to my mom, still guarding the door with Allie. I filled her in.

"How about I talk to Jennifer for a minute," my mom said.

Allie and I went into the kitchen together.

"OK," I said to Allie. "She's NOT running off to San Francisco. Not today anyway."

Allie and I looked at each other. All of a sudden we were high-fiving. Altan8 was not running off to San Francisco! We stopped her! We did it! And then I started kind of crying again and Allie kind of hugged me.

"Jamie," she said, "that was so incredibly IS."

33

They were all gone! The Evil Clique of Populars was no more!!!!

"I must destroy her myself," Myrna raged. "IS MUST PAY!"

~

"Mr. Bleemos or 'Anatomy' Akins?" Malik was asking.

"Hm," Connor said. "The English teacher versus the health ed teacher . . ."

"What's your vote, Jamie?" Malik turned to me.

"What? Sorry?" I was really beat from all the excitement last night. My mom had talked to Jennifer for a long time. I was glad. I have to admit, she's great at helping people figure things out.

And then after we all went home, it was my turn to talk to my mom. And my dad. What the heck.

I poured out all of the stuff going on with me. I told them

about Harmony and Gabriela. I even spilled about Marco (NOT the kissing part). Mom just patted my hair and listened. (Well, she also told me she would deal with my date with "the Fonz" later and I was not about to get off from lying scot-free.)

Then I told them I haven't been writing. How I hadn't written practically anything except lame homework assignments and my autograph since this all started.

"The whole sequel thing?" I told them. "The essays, short stories everyone wants me to write? Even writing for school. It's all stressing me out. I know people want to see something as good as *IS*. I *love IS*, but I don't know if I can write anything even a little IS-ish!"

My mom put her arms around me.

"OK, and that's not all," I said. "People want me to write all IS, but they also want me to *be* IS! And I'm NOT!!!!"

That's when I started crying. My dad came over and hugged me, which made me cry even harder.

"Everyone looks at me and I'm a huge disappointment," I said. "I keep thinking about what this girl in Hollywood said. That my book was probably stupid because girls like me think we're standing up for something but really the mean girls always win in the end anyway so what does it matter."

"Jamie, you've seen for yourself that isn't true," my dad pointed out. "You read your fan mail—all those girls telling you about how your book has really made a difference for them."

"Well I wish it would work for *me*!"

I Flicked at the air.

"Gee," I said sarcastically. "That solved *all* my problems."

My parents looked at me. They're not big fans of sarcasm.

"Jamie, let's start by taking action. We'll help you work on cutting down on all the writing and interview requests you don't want to do," my mom said.

"Remember the attitude it took to write IS? You need to find that inside yourself again," Dad said. "You need to work on your own Flicks," added Mom.

"You guys sound like an after-school special," I grumbled.

"Just remember what's truly important, honey," Mom said. "And what's truly important is that you gave me the opportunity to meet George Jackson and his Trio."

I thought of the whole chicken-dance-on-the-piano-bar scene and gave her a look.

"Kidding!" Mom said.

"Well, *gee*, I guess it's all been worthwhile," I said, but I was smiling a little now.

"And just think about what you did for Jennifer tonight," Dad said.

Yeah, I had to give myself some credit on that one. And Allie . . . oh yeah . . .

"What was up with Allie and all the computer stuff? I mean, *Allie?*"

My parents looked at each other.

"Allie is a computer genius," Dad announced.

"What? How come I don't know this?" I asked.

"Because you are totally oblivious." Allie strolled into the room. "Who do you think changed your password to BiteMe?"

She saw the look my parents gave her. "Ooookay, forget I said that."

"While we're at it, did you apologize to Jamie for the Amazon thing I caught you doing . . . ?" my dad asked.

"Uh, not yet. OK, I was the one who wrote that bad review on Amazon.com about your book, too," Allie said. "Sorry."

"Ahhhhh! I can't believe you!" I jumped up. "I am going to kill you!!!"

"Uh-oh." Allie turned around to make an escape. "Uh— RETSIS! RETSIS! RETSIS!"

We looked at each other. And we both started to laugh.

I threw a crumpled napkin at her. Oh! The napkin reminded me. . . .

"Hang on, I forgot to give you something, Allie." I said. I ran to my bedroom and opened my dresser drawer. I pulled out the napkin I'd saved from the Teen Yes Awards after-party.

TO ALLIE,
THE FUTURE MRS. DONOVAN???
XOXOX
Ryder Donovan

~

So after all that, I was totally beat. Mom and Dad were all like, "It's late. Time for bed." I reassured them I was feeling better and headed to my bedroom. I *was* feeling better. But I couldn't sleep. I felt bad about blowing Lindsay off. I sent her

an email so at least she'd know I was thinking about her. I apologized to her for everything. Because she was right. I did ignore her a lot. I told her she deserved a better friend. And I was going to start being one. I signed off and flopped on my bed. But I still couldn't sleep.

I looked at my walls. Now would be a good time to take down Amber Tiffany. And the other supermodels and actresses that stared at me. I mean, looking at them didn't make me as crazy as it did that day I wrote *IS*. But why surround myself with that, right?

I yanked the posters down one by one. I took apart the collages. Then I pulled out a box from my closet. I took out the collage of pictures of me on a horse, me on vacation at the beach, me and Allie. I dusted off the award I won at summer camp and the good citizenship trophy. Well, maybe those could stay in the closet. But I took out my Beanie Babies and set up the pictures on my shelf where they'd been before. The purple unicorn with the sparkly horn got a special place, next to my notebooks marked "Algebra" and "History." My old journals. I hadn't journaled in forever!!!

I had been under so much pressure to write stuff for everyone else, I hadn't written anything for me. It was Journal Time. I took the cap off a glitter gel pen.

A couple things have happened since I last journaled. I found out Allie is a computer genius. I kissed a guy!!!! And I wrote a bestselling novel. Not exactly in that order . . .

34

I was going to be late to study hall, but I was on a mission. I needed to find Lindsay. I spotted her coming out of her math class.

"Jamie!" she said. "I'm so sorry I hung up on you."

"Lindsay," I said, "stop apologizing. I'm the one who should say I'm sorry. You were totally right. I was going to call you back and tell you that. But we had a family crisis that went way late."

"I'm just glad we're not fighting anymore," Lindsay said. "Are you OK? You look tired."

"I am," I told her. "Plus I was sleeping off the two bowls of cookie-dough ice cream I ate last night. I'm lucky I could squeeze into my jeans this morning."

Then Lindsay said something that took me totally by surprise. Even though it shouldn't have.

"Look, Jamie. When *you* complain about being too fat, I feel like I must be a total embarrassment. You're so way skinnier than me."

Ouch. She was right. Every time I whined about squeezing

into a pair of jeans, Lindsay must feel awful. I started to apologize but Lindsay was like, wait. She wasn't finished yet.

"I know you really don't care about other people's weight. And then when you wrote *IS* I really, really knew it! You made that one girl be the most sought-after cover girl in magazine history. Isabella was like, of COURSE she would be a cover model, she's so beautiful and oh by the way she's a plus size. So what.

"But my father, all he sees is my fat. I know it. I try to feel good about myself and then I see him looking at me like, Ugh. That's why I was calling you last night. My dad told me it looked like I put on more weight. My mom said the doctor said I was fine, I was in the healthy range. And my dad goes, Healthy like a cow."

WHOA.

"But you know what I did last night? When I couldn't talk to you, I read that part of *IS* again. And I started Flicking. And it made me feel better. This is the way my father is. Maybe I can't change it. But it doesn't mean I have to listen to it. Or believe it."

"Lindsay, you know what?" I said. "I have to say this. I know it sounds total cliché, but you seriously are a beautiful person."

I'm usually not so mushy like that, but I really meant it. I mean, Lindsay is the nicest person in the entire world. She is nice to everybody. And so what, she's not a size two. She's not magazine perfect—but she's real and, and, and . . . just a really good person.

I couldn't change her father's behavior either. I couldn't take back all the times I had complained about my own weight in front of her. But I could try to make things a little better now.

I put on my very serious I-mean-business face. I reached into my locker and got a neon green Post-it note pad.

"Your assignment is to do Isabella's Post-it note routine. Like how she writes good things about herself and then sticks them all over her bedroom. You know, like the ones my mom sticks around the house—those affirmation things? So, you do that, too. On your mirrors, on your closet door, everywhere!"

"Jamie! I can't do that," Lindsay said.

"I'm sorry, but Isabella is now turning into IS," I said. Then I told her in a gloom-and-doom voice: "You cannot disobey IS. You know what happens to those who dare disobey." I grabbed a gel pen and started to write an affirmation thingy on the top Post-it.

I have gorgeous eyes and a great smile.
I am kind to other people and deserve to
  be treated well.
I'm beautiful.

I gave the pad to Lindsay. "I could do tons more, but that's enough to get you started."

"Jamie." Lindsay was blushing, but she took the pad and the gel pen.

"Well, I think I might need to check your Post-it progress. Maybe you should invite me over this weekend to check up on you. Friday night videos at your house?"

"You're invited," Lindsay said. She turned to head to her next class but stopped and looked back at me.

"I'll do that Post-it thing if you do something, too. Flick when Sawyer is driving you nuts," Lindsay said. "And when your head is getting too big from all your success."

"Deal," I said sheepishly.

Lindsay grinned and Flicked with both hands.

35

I was sitting in study hall reading my email on my cell phone. The first one was from Jennifer2—I mean Roth.

Hi Jamie,
Thx again for everything last nite. I M
sooo glad I didn't go to San Fran. When
I told chet I wasn't coming he told me
forget it he would find someone older
and more mature. He didn't really love
me. I feel so stupid. I M not going to
school today but don't worry. Your mom
told my mom some stuff and my mom wants
me to stay home with her and talk. So
??? bye! Jen

OK. Yay!!!! I read my next email.

TedyBr: Dear IS! U kick butt! In my
school everybody was doing these slam

books. Where you put everyone's name on a notebook page and then write mean things about them like 'Chloe is a skank' and stuff. But it was my turn and I thought about IS. And I started writing NICE stuff on everyone's pages! The truth like IS would tell it! Chloe's not a skank, she's pretty and nice, so why wouldn't the guys like her!

The girl who started the slam book was really pissed. But I don't think anyone else was! ☺ Cuz then other people started writing nice stuff 2! I just wanted 2 tell u that. Paige

~

Wow. What a serious IS day. First Jennifer, then Lindsay, then these emails. Then I thought about all those other emails from girls. All those girls who had done those IS kinda things.

I should forward those to Lindsay to make her feel better. I should forward them to Jennifer.

I wish I could get those out to a lot of girls so they could read them. And that's when I thought of it. What if I could make a place for girls to share their IS stories? So everybody could get ideas about how to help themselves?

Like a website. My publisher had suggested one. They wanted me to come up with ideas. It was on my never-ending To-Do List.

Hm. Allie—secret computer genius Allie—would probably be good for ideas.

And I know Harmony, newspaper reporter, would help me write up stuff for it. And even Gabriela, OK the whole spelling-bee thing—maybe she'd want to help edit it? I'd have to ask my parents. Dad would be into it, I mean that would look good on Allie's college applications and all that. And I'd tell my mom I wasn't going to give *advice*. Like she said, I'm not able to solve people's problems. But maybe, just a little bit, I could let them tell how *they're* doing it. Cheer them on! Like, go IS girls go!!

A website . . . hm . . . .

"Earth to Jamie!" Someone was saying.

Oh! Malik was talking to me.

"So what's your answer? Bleemos or Akins?" Malik asked me impatiently.

"Oh, easy. Akins is a better teacher," I said.

"Nah," Malik said. "Who could take who in a *fight?* Bleemos or Akins?"

I was giving my answer some serious consideration, when I thought I saw Harmony's face in the window of the classroom door. I was really missing her. I wished her month in the city was over and she could come home. Well, this home.

"Isn't that Harmony Pinckney?" Connor asked.

It was! It *was* Harmony! She was waving at me to come out in the hall.

"Excuse me." I went up to the teacher's desk and talked to his face hiding behind the newspaper. "May I have the bathroom pass?"

"Scrambled" Eggleston looked at me.

"I have to *go*," I whispered, giving him the Urgent! look. He gave me the wooden pass and I went out to the hallway.

"AAAAHH! What are you doing here?!" I shrieked. Me and Harmony were jumping up and down.

"SURPRISE!" Harmony yelled. "Yes, I'm here!"

"I am sooo sorry about everything," I told her, all in a rush. "Did you get my email? And the one to give to Gabriela—"

"Yes, yes," Harmony interrupted. "It's all cool, don't worry! And guess what?! Guess who is going to be staying the school year at Whittaker High? Guess who isn't going to be shuttled back and forth every month?! Take a guess . . . Yes, it's *moi*. My mom agreed to let me stay here when there's school! Me and Beryl and my dad talked her into it last night and since she was working late, I just jumped on the train and Tada! Here I am! For good!"

Harmony was clearly excited. But I was confused. Harmony wanted to give up her beautiful room in her beautiful apartment on Central Park to come live in boring old suburbia?

"You want to leave New York City? Why?"

"Oh, I'm not *leaving* the city," she said. "I love the city. I'll be down there every school break and part of the summer.

It's just I'll be here the rest of the time. Don't worry," she added, looking at my face. "You can come with me. But Beryl told me that Kameelah is still having a hard time at school. And she sleeps with my picture at night to make her feel better. I need to be there for her. I mean, not like I can fix her alone or anything, but I know if I'm there it can only help her.

"Beryl said I could stay upstate on one condition: I stop skipping classes," Harmony added sheepishly. "I guess she's been noticing. So now she and my dad are going to be checking with my teachers. Ugh. But, hey. At least someone cares."

"But what about Raj," I asked suspiciously. "And . . . Gabriela? Won't you miss them too much?"

"Beryl said they can come and visit anytime. And I can head down some weekends. Hey, it's just a train ride away. And besides, I won't miss them as much as I missed not having *you* around!"

"Even Gabriela?" I couldn't help myself.

"Yes, Gabriela, too, you dork," Harmony said. "Gabriela's fun, but you're my best friend."

"You sure? Gabriela seems like the *perfect* friend." I still felt insecure about that girl.

Harmony rolled her eyes.

"Oh all right, you need to hear it *again*," Harmony said. "You're my BFF! You're smart, funny, genuine, creative . . . and no matter what you think, you wrote IS because you had it inside you. We might not always see it, but it's there."

"Harmony, you are seriously the best," I told her. I was so happy I couldn't stop smiling.

Oops, until "Scrambled" Eggleston opened the door.

"Miss Bartlett? Did you lose your way to the ladies' room?" he asked me.

"Um, no, I was uh, just coming back and I bumped into—" I gave Harmony a look and made a move for the classroom door.

"Miss Pinckney." Eggleston looked at her. "I believe I received a memo that you will be joining our school on a more regular basis? And doesn't that mean you should be in a class right now?"

"Yup, French. And I'm going—*really*," Harmony said, walking away down the hall. Then she turned back and yelled, "See you at lunch!"

I went back into study hall, grinning.

"Scrambled Eggleston vs. Señora Goldstein?" Malik was saying. "Who would win?"

36

IS faced Myrna, her archenemy.

"You can't change the way the world works!" Myrna sneered at IS.

And IS smiled.

"That's where you're wrong, Myrna. There are new forces at work. And the change has already begun."

~

Harmony nudged me under the table. Marco Vega was entering the cafeteria. I sat up straight. He looked around and his look stopped on me. He headed our way. Past the Popular Table and over to ours. Uh-oh. I hadn't exactly let Marco know I was over him. All of this No More Marco For Me had gone on in my own brain. Not that we were ever totally together or anything. It had been a weird relationship from the start. I hoped he wouldn't be heartbroken or anything. Just kidding.

"You OK?" Harmony whispered, seeing me watch Marco. After study hall, I'd walked with her to her locker and filled her in on my lack of feelings for Marco. He just wasn't for me, I'd told her. Oh well.

"Hey dudes," he said, sitting down. "Um, Jamie. I've got something to tell you."

"Yeah," I said. "I have something to tell you, too."

I had to tell him it wasn't working out. No more dates. No more phone conversations (Yawn!). There'd be no Jamie Bartlett Vega and 2.5 children in our future.

"I'll let you two chat," Harmony said, and left.

"This is going to sound really bad," Marco started talking first. "But I think you're a really nice girl."

"No, actually that doesn't sound bad at all," I cracked. Now that I didn't *like* him like him, I could actually speak to him. Not feeling nervous around Marco was very liberating.

"Well, what I mean is this. Um, I was hanging out with you for a reason. Sawyer kind of *made* me do it."

"But I thought you and Sawyer were over. Totally done. She was never going to speak to you again," I said.

"Oh. That," he said. "No, she calls me every night. Like seven times."

Huh?

"See," he continued. "You know Sawyer wants to be a celebrity. You know, like she did that news show and all that. But the Myrna thing wasn't getting her anywhere because people kept asking her if she was really such a bitch in real life. So she thought if you and I went out then maybe I could get famous with you. Then I would be discovered. Like a photographer or someone would say 'Jamie's boyfriend needs to be a model or an actor or something.'

(197)

"So anyway," Marco continued. "She said once I got discovered then we could lose you and I could go back with her in public. Then she could get discovered, too, and me and her would both get famous together."

"OK, huh?" I said. "I'm confused. First I got famous, so then you would get famous and then Sawyer would get famous from that?"

"I guess so," Marco said. "I wasn't really paying attention."

"That's a pretty complicated plan," I said.

"There's more," Marco said, looking down at his hands. "Then I was going to dump you, and it would be all over the news. Like Jamie's boyfriend dumps her hard for Sawyer Sullivan. And she'd look good, you'd look bad. And I was like, yeah, whatever. Just stop nagging me. Geez, she was like my mother or something."

"Um, didn't you feel bad that I was going to get the raw end in this deal?" I asked.

"See, I didn't think it would get this far," Marco said. "I thought you'd say no when I asked you out in the first place. I mean, you're all smart and a big author and I'm, you know. Into cars and stuff. But once you said yes, then Sawyer was like, You HAVE to do this and it got all messed up."

Whoa. Marco thought *I* wouldn't want to go out with *him*?

"Anyway, sorry," Marco said. "Oh, but I did want to kiss you that one time. You have cute lips."

"Well, why are you telling me all this now?" I said. "Sawyer making you do it?"

"Uh, actually Sawyer doesn't know I'm saying all this. She's going to kill me for 'breaking up' with you before she's famous. But, uh, I was talking to your friend Harmony in gym today. And how I was sick of Sawyer trying to boss me around. So Harmony told me I should tell you the truth. And that I wouldn't be breaking your heart or anything like that. So I hope you're not too pissed at me. I'm sorry, dude."

"No." I sighed. "I'm not mad at you. I know how easy it is to let Sawyer get her way . . ."

"Yeah." He kind of sighed, too.

"Well, good luck," I said, knowing full well Sawyer would be publicly back on with Marco by the end of the school day. I mean, he was the most popular guy in our grade. *And* he was serious eye candy.

I should tell Marco to read *IS*. So he could get some spine and stand up to Sawyer.

"Wait!" I said. "Shouldn't we make it so *I* dumped *you*? Then Sawyer wouldn't be so mad at you, because you didn't do anything wrong. Tell her I dumped you for, um, Ryder Donovan or something."

Yeah, that was better. It would save me a little pride. Hm, and then when he "went back" to Sawyer it would be like she was getting my leftovers. Heh, heh. OK, *so* not mature of me.

"Sure, no prob," Marco said, already taking off.

I watched him walk away toward Sawyer. He was still yummy. But I was really over him now. I Flicked Sawyer a couple times from under the table on Marco's behalf. He needed the protection.

~

Harmony, Lindsay, and I were at our lockers after lunch. Lindsay was telling us about her new idea.

"So Señora Goldstein told us about the new afterschool kickboxing class she'd be teaching," Lindsay said. "At first I was like, me, kickboxing? But then I was thinking about Isabella doing martial arts and feeling strong and powerful. And Jamie, after you talked to me about, you know, everything . . . I just made up my mind."

"That's awesome," I told her.

"And I'm not even doing it just because of the whole weight thing," Lindsay said. "I know I need to exercise, but Señora also said that it's a great way to relieve stress. You know, if my dad gets on my case then I can be like, POW! Kick! I mean, not him, of course. The punching bag.

"So, I'm going to go sign up now," Lindsay continued. "See ya."

"Go, Lindsay!" Harmony and I high-fived her as she took off.

~

I had my head in my locker to find my notebook when I heard someone going, "Moo, Moo." I looked up. I could see

Margaret Adams a couple lockers down from me. She was wearing one of her usual outfits, a long, flowy flowered dress. Her hair was in braids today.

"Hey, Laura Ingalls, Pa wants you home to milk the cows!" Sawyer was saying really loud. Jennifer1 was going, "Moo, Moo."

Harmony and I looked at each other.

"What a loser." Sawyer cracked up. "A LOOOOOSER."

OK, enough was enough.

"I've had it with that Sawyer," I heard myself saying. "I'm going to say something." I shut my locker.

"Wait," Harmony said. "Jamie, just wait a sec. Look at Margaret!"

What? Did she just mean we should stand there and watch Margaret burst into tears like she always did when Sawyer abused her?

But oh. Huh. Margaret was doing the Double Flick. The most powerful Flick for courage and strength.

Flick, Flick. Flick, Flick.

"Mooo!" Sawyer and Jennifer1 were still cracking themselves up. Then they noticed Margaret was just standing there, not moving except for her hands. And Margaret was just looking at them, like, Excuse me, but are you speaking to me?

"Mooooo!" Jennifer1 kept going. And Sawyer goes, "Something smells like cow manure! Oh, it's Margaret!" But Margaret just stood there, with a kind of smile on her face.

Sawyer looked at Margaret.

Margaret looked back at Sawyer.

Flick, Flick.

Flick, Flick.

"Oh come on, Jennifer," Sawyer snarled. "We're late for gym."

Jennifer1 started Mooing again, but Sawyer goes, "Shut up, Jennifer."

Margaret walked off the other way, and you know what, now she was really smiling. And when Sawyer and Jennifer1 were all the way around the corner, Margaret let out a big, huge laugh.

～

FLICK. FLICK.

"You're going to LOSE! You're a LOSER, IS! A LOOOOOSER!!!" Myrna screamed. And she got smaller and smaller.

Until she disappeared from the face of the Earth.

IS dusted off her hands. She turned to walk away.

And that's when she noticed a girl, who had seen the whole thing.

"Wow," said the girl. "I wish I could do that."

"Oh, but you can," IS told her. "Every girl—any girl— has the power within her to Flick."

The girl curled her hand into a fist. And then . . .

She Flicked.

37

After school, I headed out toward the buses. Harmony told me to wait for her, so I walked up the hill out front where you could see everyone leaving school. There was a wall, so I jumped up and sat on it to wait.

I was heading over to her house for the "Welcome Home, Harmony" party. And Raj was coming up from the city for the occasion. I was finally going to meet Raj! Harmony's dad was making his famous Pasta Pinckney. Maybe there'd be cake for dessert. Yum.

Maybe things were getting back to normal.

There was Allie, heading out with Duh. She saw me and waved. I waved back.

Lindsay and Malik were walking out together. It looked like she was showing him some kickboxing moves. Kick! Kick! Hm. Lindsay and Malik? Malik karate-chopped her back.

Lindsay and Malik?!!!

Yes, they were so definitely flirting.

Huh.

"Hey, Jamie Bartlett!" Oh, *great*. Sawyer Sullivan and her slave, Jennifer1, were heading my way.

"I hope you enjoyed borrowing my boyfriend for a while," Sawyer said.

"It's not like Marco ever really liked you or anything you know! He was just faking it," Jennifer1 added.

Gee, thanks for sharing.

"And Marco told me all about your kiss so don't think he keeps *any* secrets from me. Of course, he only kissed you 'cause he felt sorry for you," Sawyer said. "And it's not like he would have tried to go any farther than first base. I mean, what's the use of going to second base when there's nothing there to go for?"

"Get it? Cause you have no chest?!" Jennifer added helpfully.

Oh ha-ha-ha.

This would be a good time for a nice Double Flick.

Oh, what the heck.

Flick. Flick.

They were still laughing. I pictured Sawyer shrinking away into nothingness. I smiled at the thought. And then stopped smiling. Because I knew what I needed to do.

It had to be done. And now was the time. I jumped down off the wall.

"Hey, Sawyer," I said. "I need to talk to you for a second."

"What?" Sawyer asked suspiciously.

"In private, just for a minute," I said. Stay calm, Jamie. Stay cool. Flick. Flick.

Sawyer waved Jennifer1 away.

"OK, what. You've got five seconds," she said, looking at her watch.

I looked her right in the eye.

"I don't know why you don't like me, but OK, you don't," I told her. "Fine. But we can treat each other with some respect. OK? OK. That's all."

"You've obviously mistaken me for someone who cares," Sawyer said, with an exaggerated yawn.

"Look, we both know you've got some funny putdowns," I said. "'Why should anyone bother going to second base with you?' That's pretty funny, actually."

"What, you think you just say that, and that's going to stop me?" Sawyer said.

I looked right at her.

"Yeah. I do. You can stop . . . now," I said.

Sawyer just stood there looking like . . . What's going on here?

"I think the buses are leaving. You better go," I said, trying not to let my voice shake.

Sawyer looked at the buses. Jennifer1 had already gone ahead. Then Sawyer looked at me. She looked like she was going to say something. But then she just turned around and walked really fast. Down the hill.

I let out a huge breath. I was shaking. OMG. I can't believe I just did that.

As Sawyer walked toward her bus, farther and farther down the hill, she looked smaller and smaller.

So that's how the Double Flick worked.

OK, I'm not completely naïve. I knew Sawyer wasn't gone from my life forever. But for now at least, she was walking away.

Sawyer walked past the first bus. And all of a sudden, a fist shot out the bus window. Then out of the second bus, a couple of fists. OMG, they were Flicking Sawyer. Flick, Flick, Flick.

And Sawyer bounced on, having no clue she had left a trail of Flicking fists behind her.

OK. Maybe Kimberlee was wrong about the Myrnas always winning. Yeah, sometimes they do. But sometimes, maybe sometimes, they just *think* they do. And the rest of us, all of the rest of us, know better.

As I settled back on the wall my pager went off:

Jamie! Call me ASAP! Your book is going to be made into a movie! Leslie

OMG! My book!! *IS* was going to be made into a movie. A MOVIE! I was going to see IS on the big screen! OMG!! Who would play Isabella?! What would I wear to the premiere! OMG OMG!!!

"BOO!" I lost my balance and fell right off the wall. Backward.

Oof!

"Whoops, sorry!" Connor said, jumping over the wall and trying to help me up.

"OK, can we pretend that didn't happen?" I said, totally red-faced. I pulled myself back on the wall, mortified.

"Is this seat reserved?" Connor asked, pointing to the spot next to me.

"Well, I'm meeting Harmony any second but yeah, you can sit there until she gets here," I told him. Let's see what I can do for an encore to make a fool of myself, I thought.

I looked sideways at Connor. At this angle he kind of looked like Josh Hartnett.

"I wanted to say thanks for everything you did for Jennifer," Connor said. "She called me last night and told me what was going on. I didn't know anything about that guy. I can't believe she would have been so stupid."

"Yeah, well I don't think she was thinking straight. Her parents were really getting to her. And her so-called friends, too," I said.

"Yeah, I know," Connor said. "My mom's known Jen's mom since college. When my dad left us, that's who my mom cried to. Then when my parents got back together and we moved here, my mom started hanging out with Jen's mom again. And Jen told me about her mom and stepfather always fighting. It's pretty ugly."

"I hope it's all going to get better for her," I said.

"Yeah, me, too," Connor said. "My parents told me that her family's going to go to counseling. And they might be able to press charges or something against the Internet guy. I guess he was saying some pretty intense stuff to Jennifer. So anyway, thanks a lot for everything you did for her. I don't even want to think about what could have happened. Geez."

"Well, I didn't do all that much," I said.

"Yes, you did. I mean for starters, Jennifer emailed *you* for advice and for help," Connor said. "She's lucky you were there for her."

I thought about how I had blown off her emails for a while.

"I wasn't so helpful at first," I told him. "Now I know if I get emails like that I'm going to get someone to help me. That was so way over my head."

We sat in silence. I remembered the silence when I was with Marco. Like I couldn't think of anything to say. This felt different. Just comfortable.

"Jennifer's pretty nice, when she's not around Sawyer Sullivan. Like in our writing critique group that one day, she was nice. She's a good writer, too."

"Yeah, she is," Connor said. "I know she wants to be a writer someday. Maybe you could help her out. You know, so she learns to write better."

"Me help her?" I said. "You thought my story sucked. And hers was so great."

Connor looked at me.

"OK, my story did kind of suck," I said.

"You weren't really into what you were writing. When you care about something, your writing is amazing."

OK, I was turning red again.

"I hope Jennifer didn't hurt you too much," I blurted out.

"What?"

"You know. Because she was leaving you for another guy."

I CAN'T BELIEVE I JUST SAID THAT.

"I don't get it." Connor looked at me.

"Well, you know, leaving you to go to San Francisco to be with the Internet Creep?"

Connor just looked at me like, what was I talking about?

"Aren't you and Jennifer, you know, together?"

"Me and Jen?" Connor said. "Nah! We're just thrown together because our mothers have been friends so long. She's like a cousin or something. Anyway, she's not my type."

"Oh. It's just you guys seem close. Always class partners, you know. All that," I said.

"She needed someone to talk to," Connor said. "And she didn't have to pretend everything was OK with me. But there's nothing going on with us or anything."

OH.

"One thing's for sure, she's definitely got to break away from Sawyer," he said.

I thought about my friends. Lindsay and, of course, Harmony. They stuck by me no matter what. And how Jennifer didn't even have parents she could count on.

I tuned back in to what Connor was saying.

"You know if Jennifer could spend a little time with you and your friends, maybe she'd figure that out," Connor said. "You guys might be a good influence on her."

"Thanks!" I said. That was a nice thing to say.

"Wow, did *you* just say thanks?" Connor teased me.

"Oh. I guess I do have a hard time taking compliments," I admitted.

"Well, we'll just have to work on that. We'll practice. Here: You're funny. You're an awesome writer. And you have really nice eyes."

I looked at him. "Really? You think I have nice eyes?" I squeaked. He had nice eyes, too. Nice a lot of things.

"Yeah, I like your eyes," Connor said. "A lot."

He was looking really hard at me. I was holding my breath. I looked away and saw—THE BUSES! The buses were leaving! I saw the first bus start to pull out.

"I gotta catch my bus!!!" I said. "I'm supposed to meet . . . "

Hey, wait a minute. There was Harmony, hanging out the bus window and waving at me. What the—

"Actually," Connor said. "I hope you don't mind but I kind of asked Harmony if I could give you a ride to her house. I mean, if my sister could. She's home from college on break. Harmony's place is on her way, so she said she'd swing by and give me a ride. And you, too. If that's okay."

Why had I never noticed how *nice* Connor really was?

OK, how many times could I use the word NICE about someone. And he was more than just nice, he was smart and he was a good listener and he was really confident and . . . I was starting to sound like Harmony talking about Raj now.

"Thanks for offering me the ride," I said. I guess he'd planned that so he could have a chance to talk to me about Jennifer in private.

"You know, if you want to, I could have my sister give you a ride home this week, like whenever she's taking me. I mean, if you want me to. I mean, if you have something going on after school I wouldn't, but on other days. You know instead of the bus. And then, if you want, you could sometimes stop at my house and we could hang or watch a video or something." That all came out in kind of a rush. Connor suddenly sounded not so much like his usual confident self.

Does that mean what I think it might mean? ????

"OK! Yeah!" I couldn't really meet his eye, so I pulled my backpack on and then jumped off the wall. Or tried to, anyway.

Oof!

I fell backward off the wall. Again. Great. I'm on the ground on my back weighed down by my 250-pound backpack. Connor's face appeared over the wall.

"Are you OK?" he asked, all concerned.

Oh, what the heck.

"No, I'm not OK," I said out loud and confessed right to Connor. "I'm *totally humiliated*. But Isabella would say to laugh this off. Like if it happened to someone else, I would think it's funny, right? So I'm supposed to think it's funny even if it happened to me and just laugh about it. SO ha-ha-ha," I grumbled.

"Well. It was pretty funny." Great. Connor is trying not to crack up. It's not working. He's cracking up.

OK, I started cracking up, too. It was a teeny, tiny, little bit funny. Connor kind of pulled me up to my feet. And held my hands for one second longer than he needed to.

"I think we'd better find you a safer seat," Connor said,

pointing to a little sports car pulling up. "You and I will have to squeeze in the back. I hope you don't mind squishing a little."

~

Pop Quiz:

**If you could be squished in a car
with one person from Whittaker High,
who would you choose?**

A. Marco Vega
B. The Kid Who Stole the
   Dissected Frog from Biology
C. Sawyer Sullivan (*just kidding*)
D. Connor Griffin

~

"The way it should be, is the way it now IS."

Hee.

Thank You to . . .

My twin sister, Jennifer Roy ☆ Rebecca Sherman at Writers House ☆ Susan Cohen, my literary agent at Writers House ☆ Meredith Mundy Wasinger, my editor, and everyone else at Dutton Children's Books, especially Doug Whiteman, Stephanie Owens Lurie, Margaret Woollatt, Heather Wood, Andrea Mosbacher, Suzanne Lander, Rosanne Lauer, Diane Giddis, Laurence Tucci, Jennifer Miller, and the marketing, sales and publicity departments ☆ Mona Daly ☆ Julie Kane-Ritsch at The Gotham Group ☆ David DeVillers ☆ Quinn DeVillers ☆ Jack DeVillers ☆ Amy Rozines ☆ Melissa Weichmann ☆ Dawn Nocera ☆ Megan McCafferty ☆ Sonya Sones ☆ Les Armour ☆ Johannah Haney ☆ Eloise DiPietra ☆ Roy Carlisle ☆ Harmony Tapper ☆ And all my readers!!!